Learn to Speak Klingon Like a Native with Easy Phrases Like:

What do you want?   —nuqneH
  (greeting)   (pronounced nook-NEKH)

That is unfortunate.   —Do'Ha'
                        (pronounced do-KHA)

I don't understand.   —jIyajbe'
                        (pronounced ji-YAJ-be)

It's not my fault.   —pIch vIghajbe'
                        (pronounced pich vi-ghaj-BE)

Beam me aboard!   —HIjol
                        (pronounced khi-JOL)

THE
KLINGON
DICTIONARY
ENGLISH/KLINGON
KLINGON/ENGLISH

By MARC OKRAND

**Based on the Klingon language in
STAR TREK® and
STAR TREK: THE NEXT GENERATION®**

POCKET BOOKS
New York   London   Toronto   Sydney

An *Original* publication of Pocket Books

POCKET BOOKS, a division of Simon & Schuster Inc.
1230 Avenue of the Americas, New York, NY 10020

STAR TREK is a Registered Trademark of Paramount Pictures.

This book is published by Pocket Books, a division of Simon & Schuster Inc. under exclusive license from Paramount Pictures.

ISBN-13: 978-0-671-74559-2
ISBN-10:   0-671-74559-X

First Pocket Books trade paperback printing January 1992

40 39

CONTENTS

INTRODUCTION

Klingon is the official language of the Klingon Empire. For a long time, only a few non-Klingons were able to learn enough about the language to engage in a meaningful conversation with a Klingon. Recently, however, under the auspices of the Federation Scientific Research Council, a study has been undertaken to record and analyze the language and culture of the Klingons, with the ultimate goal of preparing an encyclopedia, as well as teaching materials. This dictionary represents the initial results of that effort.

The dictionary is divided into two main parts: grammatical sketch and dictionary proper.

The grammatical sketch is intended to be an outline of Klingon grammar, not a complete description. Nevertheless, it should allow the reader to put Klingon words together in an acceptable manner. Many of the rules given in the grammatical sketch are those set down by Klingon grammarians. It should be remembered that even though the rules say "always" and "never," when Klingon is actually spoken these rules are sometimes broken. What the rules represent, in other words, is what Klingon grammarians agree on as the "best" Klingon.

Because research is not yet completed, this dictionary is of necessity somewhat limited in scope. There are certainly more Klingon words than those listed here. Three groups of words in particular are, for the most part, unrepresented: scientific terminology; words for native tools, customs, flora, and fauna; and vocabulary dealing with food. Terms associated with the various sciences are the subject of a special study, and a report is currently being prepared. Klingon words for traditional tools and long-standing customs are difficult to translate into English. Native plants and animals are likewise difficult to comprehend at the present time. Such matters will be fully elucidated in the forthcoming *Klingon Encyclopedia.* Food words are missing due to limited resources: there have been problems recruiting staff interested in studying Klingon eating habits. Until that study is under way, it was thought inappropriate to present a list of words whose meanings are not properly understood.

As more data are gathered the list of words will undoubtedly grow. Even at this early stage, however, some patterns are emerging. For example, there are no words for greetings, such as *hello, how are you, good morning,* and so on. It seems apparent that such words and phrases simply do not exist in Klingon. When two Klingons meet each other (except in cases where military protocol determines behavior), if anything of an introductory nature is said, it is an expression that can best be translated as *What do you want?* Unlike most speakers of English, who begin conversations with greetings, inquiries about the state of health of the conversants, and remarks about the weather, Klingons tend to begin conversations by simply stating the main points.

Although Klingons are proud of their language and frequently engage in long discussions about its expressiveness and beauty, they have found it impractical for communication outside the Klingon Empire. For intra- and intergalactic communication, the Klingon government, along with most other governments, has accepted English as the lingua franca. In general, only those Klingons of the upper classes (which include higher-level governmental and military officials) learn English. As a result, English has taken on two additional functions in Klingon society. First, it is used as a symbol of rank or status. Those Klingons who know English will use it among themselves to show off their erudition and make their place in society known to all who happen to be listening. Second, English is used when it is thought best to keep servants, soldiers, or even the general populace uninformed. Thus, on a Klingon vessel, the commanding officer will often speak Klingon when giving orders to his crew, but choose English when having discussions with his officers. On the other hand, a Klingon officer may use Klingon in the presence of non-Klingons to prevent them from knowing what is going on. This use of Klingon seems to be quite effective.

There are a number of dialects of Klingon. Only one of the dialects, that of the current Klingon emperor, is represented in this dictionary. When a Klingon emperor is replaced, for whatever reason, it has historically been the case that the next emperor speaks a different dialect. As a result, the new emperor's dialect becomes the official dialect. Those Klingons who do not speak the official dialect are considered either stupid or subversive, and are usually forced to undertake tasks that speakers of the official dialect find distasteful. Most Klingons try to be fluent in several dialects.

Some dialects differ only slightly from the dialect of this dictionary. Differences tend to be in vocabulary (the word for *forehead,* for example, is different in almost every dialect) and in the pronunciation of a few sounds. On the other hand, some dialects differ significantly from the current official dialect, so much so that speakers of these dialects have a great deal of difficulty communicating with current Klingon officialdom. The student of Klingon is warned to check into the political situation of the Klingon Empire before trying to talk.

There is a native writing system for Klingon (called **pIqaD**) which seems to be well suited to the various dialects. This writing system is not yet well understood and is, therefore, not used in this dictionary. Instead, a transcription system based on the English alphabet has been devised. An article is being prepared for the *Klingon Encyclopedia* which will explain the details of **pIqaD.**

In the grammatical sketch portion of this dictionary, as a notational convention, Klingon will be written in boldface type, and English translations will be written in italics: **tlhIngan** *Klingon.*

The author would like to thank the Scientific Research Council for making funds available to carry out this research, as well as various members of the Federation Interlanguage

Institute who were quite helpful in criticizing earlier drafts of the dictionary. The author apologizes for any mistakes, and sincerely hopes that none of them leads to any unfortunate misunderstandings.

Finally, a great deal of credit must be given to the Klingon informant who provided all of the data upon which this dictionary is based. Although a prisoner of the Federation, he worked long, hard hours to make his knowledge available to citizens of the Federation. Maltz, we thank you.

1. THE SOUNDS OF KLINGON

It is difficult to describe accurately the sounds of the Klingon language without using complex phonological and anatomical terminology. What follows, therefore, is intended to give only a guide to pronunciation. The best way to learn to pronounce Klingon with no trace of a Terran or other accent is to become friends with a group of Klingons and spend a great deal of time socializing with them. Very few non-Klingons speak Klingon without an accent.

The system of writing Klingon used in this dictionary has been developed so people who already know how to read English will have a minimum of difficulty approximating the sounds of Klingon words and sentences.

1.1. Consonants

b As in English *bronchitis* or *gazebo*. Some Klingons pronounce this sound as if it were **m** and **b** articulated almost simultaneously. Speakers of English can approximate this sound by saying *imbalance* without the initial *i* sound. A very small number of Klingons pronounce **b** as if it were **m**.

ch As in English *chew* or *artichoke*.

D This sound is close to English *d* in *dream* or *android*, but it is not quite the same. The English *d* sound is made by touching the tip of the tongue to that part of the roof of the mouth just behind the upper teeth. Klingon **D** can best be approximated by English-speakers by touching the tip of the tongue to the roof of the mouth at a point about halfway between the teeth and the velum (or soft palate), that part of the roof of the mouth that is rather gooshy. As with Klingon **b,** some speakers pronounce **D** as if it were more like *nd,* and a distinct minority as if it were **n**—but, of course, with the tongue in the same position as for **D.**

gh This is not like anything in English. It can be produced by putting the tongue in the same position it would be in to say English *g* as in *gobble,* but relaxing the tongue somewhat and humming. It is the same as Klingon **H** (see below), but with the vocal cords vibrating at the same time.

H This is also not like anything in English, but it is just like *ch* in the name of the German composer *Bach* or in the Yiddish toast *l'chaim,* or the *j* in the Mexican city of *Tijuana* in *Baja California.* It is produced in the same way as Klingon **gh,** but is articulated with a very coarse, strong rasp. Unlike Klingon **gh,** the vocal cords do not vibrate in saying Klingon **H.**

j As in English *junk;* never ever as in French *jour.*

l As in English *lunge* or *alchemy.*

m As in English *mud* or *pneumatic.* Those few Klingons who pronounce **b** as **m** would say Klingon **baH** *fire (a torpedo)* and **maH** *we* the same way, and have to memorize which word is spelled which way.

n As in English *nectarine* or *sunspot.* Those Klingons who pronounce **D** more like **n** can easily articulate and hear the two sounds differently. Even a **D** that sounds like **n** is pronounced with the tongue in the Klingon **D** position, not in the English *d* position. Klingon **n** is produced with the tongue in the same position as English *d.*

ng As in English *furlong;* never as in English *engulf.* The *g* is never pronounced as a separate sound. This sound never occurs at the beginning of an English word, but it does come at the beginning of a number of Klingon words. English-speakers may practice making this sound at the beginning of a word by saying English *dang it!,* then saying it again without the *da.*

p As in English *parallax* or *opprobrium.* It is always articulated with a strong puff or pop, never laxly. Speakers of English may want to exercise care to avoid discharging saliva while articulating this sound. It should be noted, however, that Klingons do not worry about this.

q Similar to English *k* in *kumquat,* but not quite that. The tongue position for English *k* is like that for Klingon **gh** and **H.** To produce Klingon **q,** the main body of the tongue touches the roof of the mouth at a point farther back than it does for **gh** or **H.** Indeed, the tongue reaches for or touches the uvula (the fleshy blob that dangles down from the back of the roof of the mouth), so articulating **q** approximates the sound of choking. The sound is usually accompanied by a slight puff of air. English speakers are reminded that Klingon **q** is never pronounced *kw* as in the beginning of English *quagmire.*

Q This is like nothing particularly noteworthy in English. It is an overdone Klingon **q.** It is identical to **q** except that it is very guttural and raspy and strongly articulated, somewhat like a blend of Klingon **q** and **H.**

r This is not like the *r* in American English, but it does resemble the *r* in some dialects of British English, as well as the *r* in many languages of Europe. It is lightly trilled or rolled.

S This sound is halfway between English *s* and *sh,* as in *syringe* and *shuttlecock.* It is made with the tip of the tongue reaching toward that part of the roof of the mouth which it touches to produce Klingon **D.**

t As in English *tarpaulin* or *critique.* It differs from Klingon **D** in two ways: (1) like **p,** it is accompanied by a puff of air; and (2) the tongue touches a position on the roof of the mouth farther forward than that for **D.**

tlh This sound does not occur in English, but it is very much like the final sound in *tetl,* the Aztec word for *egg,* if properly pronounced. To produce this sound, the tip of the tongue touches the same part of the roof of the mouth it touches for **t,** the sides of the tongue are lowered away from the side upper teeth, and air is forced through the space on both sides between tongue and teeth. The sound is produced with a great deal of friction, and the warning given in the description of Klingon **p** might be aptly repeated here.

v As in English *vulgar* or *demonstrative.*

15

w Usually as in English *worrywart* or *cow*. On rare occasions, especially if the speaker is being rather deliberate, it is pronounced strongly, more like **Hw** or even **Huw.**

y As in English *yodel* or *joy*.

' The apostrophe indicates a sound which is frequently uttered, but not written, in English. It is a glottal stop, the slight catch in the throat between the two syllables of *uh-oh* or *unh-unh,* meaning "no." When Klingon **'** comes at the end of a word, the vowel preceding the **'** is often repeated in a very soft whisper, as if an echo. Thus, Klingon **je'** *feed* almost sounds like **je'e,** where the articulation of the first **e** is abruptly cut off by the **',** and the second **e** is a barely audible whisper. When **'** follows **w** or **y** at the end of a word, there is often a whispered, echoed **u** or **I,** respectively. Occasionally the echo is quite audible, with a guttural sound like **gh** preceding the echoed vowel. For example, **yIII'** *transmit it!* can sound more like **yIII'ghI.** This extra-heavy echo is heard most often when the speaker is particularly excited or angry.

1.2. Vowels

There are five vowels in Klingon.

a As in English *psalm;* never as in American English *crabapple.*

e As in English *sensor.*

I As English *i* in *misfit.* Once in a while, it is pronounced like *i* in *zucchini,* but this is very rare and it is not yet known exactly what circumstances account for it.

o As in English *mosaic.*

u As in English *gnu* or *prune;* never as in *but* or *cute.*

Note that when a vowel is followed by **w** or **y**, the combination of letters may not represent the same sound it does in English spelling:

KLINGON	RHYMES WITH ENGLISH	AS IN
aw	*ow*	*cow*
ay	*y*	*cry*
ey	*ay*	*pay*

| Iy | ey | key |
| oy | oy | toy |

Klingon **uy** resembles *ooey* in English *gooey*. Klingon **ew** resembles nothing in English, but can be approximated by running Klingon **e** and **u** together. Likewise, Klingon **Iw** is **I** and **u** run together. No words in Klingon have **ow** or **uw**. If they did, they would be indistinguishable from words ending in **o** and **u**, respectively.

1.3. Stress

Each Klingon word of more than one syllable normally contains one stressed (or accented) syllable. The stressed syllable is pronounced at a slightly higher pitch and with a little more force than the nonstressed syllable(s).

In a verb, the stressed syllable is usually the verb itself, as opposed to any prefix or suffix. If, however, a suffix ending with ' is separated from the verb by at least one other suffix, both the verb and the suffix ending in ' are stressed. In addition, if the meaning of any particular suffix is to be emphasized, the stress may shift to that syllable. Suffixes indicating negation or emphasis (section 4.3) are frequently stressed, as is the interrogative suffix (section 4.2.9).

In a noun, the stressed syllable is usually the syllable right before the first noun suffix, or the final syllable if there is no suffix. If, however, a syllable ending in ' is present, it is usually stressed instead. If there are two syllables in a row both ending in ', both are equally stressed.

Finally, it should be noted that there are some words which seem to have variable stress patterns, with the stress sometimes heard on one syllable and sometimes on another. This phenomenon is not yet understood. The rules given above do not account for this variability, but if they are followed, stress will wind up on acceptable syllables.

In the system used to transcribe Klingon in this dictionary, stress is not indicated.

2. GRAMMATICAL SKETCH—INTRODUCTION

It is not possible, in a brief guide such as this, to describe the grammar of Klingon completely. What follows is only a sketch or outline of Klingon grammar. Although a good many of the fine points are not covered, the sketch will allow the student of Klingon to figure out what a Klingon is saying and to respond in an intelligible, though somewhat brutish, manner. Most Klingons will never know the difference.

There are three basic parts of speech in Klingon: *noun, verb,* and *everything else.*

3. NOUNS

There are various types of nouns in Klingon.

3.1. Simple nouns

Simple nouns, like simple nouns in English, are simple words; for example, **DoS** *target* or **QIH** *destruction*.

3.2. Complex nouns

Complex nouns, on the other hand, are made up of more than one part.

3.2.1. Compound nouns

Compound nouns consist of two or three nouns in a row, much like English *earthworm (earth* plus *worm)* or *password (pass* plus *word)*. For example, **jolpa'** *transport room* consists of **jol** *transport beam* plus **pa'** *room*.

3.2.2. Verb plus -wI'

A second type of complex noun consists of a verb followed by a suffix meaning *one who does* or *thing which does*. The English suffix *-er* (as in *builder* "one who builds" or *toaster* "thing which toasts") is a rough equivalent. In Klingon, the suffix is **-wI'**. It occurs, for example, in **baHwI'** *gunner,* which consists of the verb **baH** *fire (a torpedo)* plus **-wI'** *one who does.* Thus, **baHwI'** is literally "one who fires [a torpedo]." Similarly, **So'wI'** *cloaking device* comes from the verb **So'** *cloak* plus **-wI'** *thing which does.* **So'wI'** is a "thing which cloaks."

A noun formed by adding **-wI'** to a verb is a regular noun, so it may be used along with another noun to form a compound noun. For example, **tIjwI'ghom** *boarding party* comes from **tIjwI'** *boarder* plus **ghom** *group;* and **tIjwI'** comes from **tIj** *board* plus **-wI'**.

3.2.3. Other complex nouns

There are a good many nouns in Klingon which are two or, less frequently, three syllables long, but which are not complex nouns of the types described above. These nouns probably at one time were formed by combining simple nouns, but one or all of the nouns forming the complex noun are no longer in use, so it is not possible (without extensive etymological research) to know what the individual pieces mean.

For example, **'ejDo'** means *starship.* The syllable **'ej** also occurs in **'ejyo'** *Starfleet.* There are, however, no known Klingon words **'ej, Do',** or **yo'** that have anything to do with Starfleet, starships, the Federation, or space vehicles of any kind. It is quite likely that **Do'** is an Old Klingon word for *space vessel* (the modern Klingon word is **Duj**) that is used nowhere except in the noun **'ejDo'**. Of course, without further study, that remains pure conjecture.

3.3. Suffixes

All nouns, whether simple or complex, may be followed by one or more suffixes. If there are two or more suffixes, the suffixes must occur in a specific order. Suffixes may be classified on the basis of their relative order after the noun. There are five types of suffixes (which, for convenience, will be numbered 1 through 5). Suffixes of Type 1 come right after the noun; suffixes of Type 2 come after those of Type 1; suffixes of Type 5 come last. This may be illustrated as follows:

Of course, if no suffix of Type 1 is used but a suffix of Type 2 is used, the Type 2 suffix comes right after the noun. If a suffix of Type 5 is the only suffix used, it comes right after the noun. Only when two or more suffixes are used does their order become apparent.

There are at least two suffixes in each suffix type. Only one suffix of each type may be used at a time. That is, a noun cannot be followed by, for example, two or three Type 4 suffixes.

The members of each suffix type are as follows.

3.3.1. Type 1: Augmentative/diminutive

-'a' *augmentative*

This suffix indicates that what the noun refers to is bigger, more important, or more powerful than it would be without the suffix.

SuS *wind, breeze*	**SuS'a'** *strong wind*
Qagh *mistake*	**Qagh'a'** *major blunder*
woQ *power*	**woQ'a'** *ultimate power*

-Hom *diminutive*

This is the opposite of the augmentative suffix. It indicates that what the noun refers to is smaller, less important, or less powerful than it would be without the suffix.

SuS *wind, breeze*	**SuSHom** *wisp of air*
roj *peace*	**rojHom** *truce, temporary peace*

3.3.2. Type 2: Number

As in English, a singular noun in Klingon has no specific suffix indicating that it is singular: **nuH** *weapon* refers to a single weapon of any type. Unlike English, however, the lack of a specific suffix for plural does not always indicate that the noun is singular. In Klingon, a noun without a plural suffix may still refer to more than one entity. The plurality is indicated by a pronoun, whether a verb prefix (see section 4.1) or a full word (section 5.1), or by context. For example, **yaS** *officer* may refer to a single officer or to a group of officers, depending on other words in the sentence or the context of the discussion.

Compare:

> **yaS vImojpu'** *I became an officer.*
> **yaS DImojpu'** *We became officers.*

> **yaS jIH** *I am an officer.*
> **yaS maH** *We are officers.*

In the first pair of sentences, the only difference is the verb prefix (here only partially described; see section 4.1): **vI-** *I*, **DI-** *we*. In the second pair, the pronouns are different: **jIH** *I*, **maH** *we*.

Under certain circumstances, the only way to know whether the noun refers to one or more than one entity is by context. Thus, **yaS mojpu'** can be translated either *he/she became an officer* or *they became officers*. Those taking part in any discussion in which this sentence is used would presumably already know whom is being talked about, so they would also know whether *he* or *she* or *they* is the correct meaning.

Fortunately for students of Klingon, it is never incorrect to add a plural suffix to a noun referring to more than one entity, even in those cases where it is unnecessary to do so. Accordingly, both **yaS maH** and **yaSpu' maH** are correct, both meaning *we are officers* (**-pu'** is a plural suffix). On the other hand, a plural suffix cannot be added to a noun referring to only one thing, even if pronouns are present in the sentence. In Klingon, **yaSpu' jIH** *I am officers* is as incorrect as its English translation.

There are three different plural suffixes in Klingon.

-pu' *plural for beings capable of using language*

This suffix can be used to indicate plurality for Klingons, Terrans, Romulans, Vulcans, and so on, but not for lower animals of any kind, plants, inanimate objects, electromagnetic or other beams or waves, etc.

NOUNS

yaS *officer*　　　　　　　　　**yaSpu'** *officers*
Duy *emissary*　　　　　　　　**Duypu'** *emissaries*

-Du' *plural for body parts*

This suffix is used when referring to body parts of those beings capable of using language as well as of any other animal.

qam *foot*　　　　　　　　　　**qamDu'** *feet*
tlhon *nostril*　　　　　　　　**tlhonDu'** *nostrils*

-mey *plural, general usage*

This suffix is used to mark the plural of any noun.

mID *colony*　　　　　　　　　**mIDmey** *colonies*
yuQ *planet*　　　　　　　　　**yuQmey** *planets*

It can also be used with nouns referring to beings capable of using language (those nouns which take **-pu'**). When it is so used, it adds a notion of "scattered all about" to the meaning. Compare:

　　　puq *child*
　　　puqpu' *children*
　　　puqmey *children all over the place*

The suffix **-mey** cannot be used with body parts. It should be noted, however, that Klingon poets often violate this grammatical rule in order to evoke particular moods in their poetry. Thus, forms such as **tlhonmey** *nostrils scattered all about* do occur. Until the subtle nuances of such constructions are firmly grasped, however, it is suggested that students of Klingon stick to the rules.

Finally, some nouns in Klingon are inherently or always plural in meaning, and therefore never take plural suffixes.

　　　　　ray' *targets*

23

> **cha** *torpedoes*
> **chuyDaH** *thrusters*

The singular counterparts of such words are utterly distinct:

> **DoS** *target*
> **peng** *torpedo*
> **vIj** *thruster*

The singular forms may take the **-mey** suffix, but the meaning always carries the "scattered all about" connotation:

> **DoSmey** *targets scattered all about*
> **pengmey** *torpedoes all over the place*

Inherently plural nouns are treated grammatically as singular nouns in that singular pronouns are used to refer to them (sections 4.1, 5.1). For example, in the sentence **cha yIghuS** *Stand by torpedoes!* or *Get the torpedoes ready to be fired!* the verb prefix **yI-**, an imperative prefix used for singular objects, must be used even though the object (**cha** *torpedoes*) has a plural meaning.

3.3.3. Type 3: Qualification

Suffixes of this type indicate the speaker's attitude toward the noun, or how sure the speaker is that the noun is being used appropriately.

-qoq *so-called*

This suffix indicates that the noun is being used in a false or ironic fashion. Saying **rojqoq** *so-called peace,* rather than simply **roj** *peace,* indicates that the speaker does not really believe that peace is legitimate or likely to endure.

-Hey *apparent*

This suffix indicates that the speaker is pretty sure the object referred to by the noun is accurately described by the noun, but has some doubts. For example, if the scanner on a Klingon ship senses an object, and the officer reporting the presence of this object assumes, but is not yet sure, that the object is a vessel, he will probably refer to the object as **DujHey** *an apparent vessel,* rather than simply **Duj** *vessel.*

-na' *definite*

This is the counterpart of **-Hey.** It indicates that there is no doubt in the speaker's mind as to the accuracy of his or her choice of words. Once the Klingon officer referred to above is sure that the object the scanner has found is a vessel, he might report the presence of **Dujna'** *a definite vessel, undoubtedly a vessel.*

3.3.4. Type 4: Possession/specification

Type 4 is the largest class of noun suffixes. It consists of all the possessive suffixes, plus suffixes which can be translated as English *this* and *that.*

The possessive suffixes are:

-wIj *my*	**-maj** *our*
-lIj *your*	**-raj** *your (plural)*
-Daj *his, her, its*	**-chaj** *their*

Thus, **juH** *home* occurs in **juHwIj** *my home*, **juHlIj** *your home*, **juHchaj** *their home*, etc.

When the noun being possessed refers to a being capable of using language, a special set of suffixes is used for first- and second-person possessors:

-wI' *my*	**-ma'** *our*
-lI' *your*	**-ra'** *your (plural)*

These suffixes occur in, for example, **joHwI'** *my lord* and **puqlI'** *your child.* It is grammatically correct to use the regular possessive suffixes with nouns referring to beings capable of speech (as in **puqlIj** *your child*), but such constructions are considered derogatory; **joHwIj** for *my lord* borders on the taboo. Students of Klingon should bear this in mind.

To indicate that one noun is the possessor of another noun (e.g., *enemy's weapon*), no suffix is used. Instead, the two nouns are said in the order possessor–possessed: **jagh nuH** *enemy's weapon* (literally, *enemy weapon*). This construction is also used for phrases translated by *of the* in English, such as *weapon of the enemy.* (See also section 3.4.)

There are two suffixes indicating how close to the speaker the object referred to by the noun is.

-vam *this*

Like its English translation, this suffix indicates that the noun refers to an object which is nearby or which is the topic of the conversation.

nuHvam *this weapon (near me as I speak)*
yuQvam *this planet (that we've been talking about)*

When used with a plural noun (one with a plural suffix or an inherently plural noun), **-vam** is translated *these:*

nuHmeyvam *these weapons*
-vetlh *that*

This suffix indicates that the noun refers to an object which is not nearby or which is being brought up again as the topic of conversation.

nuHvetlh *that weapon (over there)*
yuQvetlh *that planet (as opposed to the one we were just talking about)*

When used with a plural noun, **-vetlh** is translated *those:*

nuHmeyvetlh *those weapons*

There is no Klingon equivalent for English *a, an, the.* In translating from Klingon to English, one must use context as a guide to when to use *a* or *an* and when *the.* In this book, *a* or *an* and *the* are used in translations to make the English sound more natural.

3.3.5. Type 5: Syntactic markers

These suffixes indicate something about the function of the noun in the sentence. As in English, subjects and objects are normally indicated by the position of the noun or nouns in the sentence. The following two English sentences have the same words, but the sentences have different meanings due to the order of the words:

Dogs chase cats.
Cats chase dogs.

26

Subjects and objects in Klingon are likewise indicated by word order. This is described in section 6.1.

In other instances, English indicates the function of nouns in a sentence by adding words, particularly prepositions. In the following English sentence, the word *around* before *canaries* indicates that the canaries are neither chasing nor being chased:

> *Dogs chase cats around canaries.*

Similarly, in Klingon, nouns which indicate something other than subject or object usually must have some special indication of exactly what their function is. Unlike English, this is accomplished by using suffixes.

-Daq *locative*

This suffix indicates that something is happening (or has happened or will happen) in the vicinity of the noun to which it is attached. It is normally translated by an English preposition: *to, in, at, on.* The exact translation is determined by the meaning of the whole sentence. For example, **pa'Daq** is **pa'** *room* plus the suffix **-Daq.** It may occur in sentences such as the following:

> **pa'Daq jIHtaH** *I'm in the room.*
> **pa'Daq yIjaH** *Go to the room!*

In the first sentence, **jIH** *I* is used in the sense of *I am* (see section 6.3), so *in* is the most reasonable translation of **-Daq.** In the second sentence, the verb is **jaH** *go,* so *to* makes the most sense as a translation of **-Daq.** An English preposition need not be part of the translation. Klingon **Dung** means *area above,* and **DungDaq** is *overhead,* literally something like "at the area above." For further discussion on prepositional concepts, see section 3.4.

It is worth noting at this point that the concepts expressed by the English adverbs *here, there,* and *everywhere* are expressed by nouns in Klingon: **naDev** *hereabouts,* **pa'** *thereabouts,* **Dat** *everywhere.* These words may perhaps be translated more literally as "area around here," "area over there," and "all places," respectively. Unlike other nouns, these three words are never followed by the locative suffix. (Note that **pa'** *thereabouts* and **pa'** *room* are identical in sound; **pa'Daq,** however, can mean only *in/to the room*.)

There are a few verbs whose meanings include locative notions, such as **ghoS** *approach, proceed*. The locative suffix need not be used on nouns which are the objects of such verbs.

> **Duj ghoStaH** *It is approaching the ship.*
> (**Duj** *ship, vessel,* **ghoStaH** *it is approaching it*)
> **yuQ wIghoStaH** *We are proceeding toward the planet.*
> (**yuQ** *planet,* **wIghoStaH** *we are proceeding toward it*)

If the locative suffix is used with such verbs, the resulting sentence is somewhat redundant, but not out-and-out wrong.

> **DujDaq ghoStaH** *It is approaching toward the ship.*

-vo' *from*

This suffix is similar to **-Daq** but is used only when action is in a direction away from the noun suffixed with **-vo'.**

> **pa'vo' yIjaH** *Leave the room!*

A more literal translation of this sentence might be "Go from the room."

-mo' *due to, because of*

This suffix occurs in sentences such as:

> **SuSmo' joqtaH** *It is fluttering in the breeze.*

The noun **SuSmo'** means *due to the breeze,* so the whole sentence is literally "due to the breeze, it [a flag] is fluttering."

-vaD *for, intended for*

This suffix indicates that the noun to which it is attached is in some way the beneficiary of the action, the person or thing for whom or for which the activity occurs.

> **Qu'vaD lI' De'vam** *This information is useful for the mission.*

The noun **Qu'vaD** means *for the mission,* and in this sentence **-vaD** indicates that the information is intended to be used somehow for the mission under discussion.

-'e' *topic*

This suffix emphasizes that the noun to which it is attached is the topic of the sentence. In English, this is frequently accomplished by stressing the noun (saying it emphatically) or by special syntactic constructions.

lujpu' jIH'e' *I, and only I, have failed.*
  It is I who has failed.
De''e' vItlhapnISpu' *I needed to get the INFORMATION.*
  It was the information (and not something else) that I needed.

Without the **'e'**, these same sentences would have no noun singled out for emphasis:

  lujpu' jIH *I have failed.*
  De' vItlhapnISpu' *I needed to get the information.*

For a further use of **-'e'**, see section 6.3.

3.3.6. Relative ordering of the suffixes

As briefly illustrated in the discussion of **-vam** *this* and **-vetlh** *that* (section 3.3.4), when a noun is followed by more than one suffix, the suffixes must occur in the proper order, according to the classification just described. It is rare for a noun to be followed by five suffixes, but it does happen from time to time. Some examples of nouns with two or more suffixes follow. (Suffix types are indicated by numbers.)

QaghHommeyHeylIjmo' *due to your apparent minor errors*

Qagh	(noun)	*error*
-Hom	(1)	*diminutive*
-mey	(2)	*plural*
-Hey	(3)	*apparent*
-lIj	(4)	*your*
-mo'	(5)	*due to*

pa'wIjDaq *in my quarters*

pa'	(noun)	*room*

29

| -wIj | (4) | *my* |
| -Daq | (5) | *locative* |

Duypu'qoqchaj *their so-called emissaries*

Duy	(noun)	*emissary*
-pu'	(2)	*plural*
-qoq	(3)	*so-called*
-chaj	(4)	*their*

qamDu'wIjDaq *at my feet*

qam	(noun)	*foot*
-Du'	(2)	*plural*
-wIj	(4)	*my*
-Daq	(5)	*locative*

rojHom'e' *the truce* (as topic)

roj	(noun)	*peace*
-Hom	(1)	*diminutive*
-'e'	(5)	*topic*

All examples of suffixes given so far show only simple nouns. Suffixes are attached to complex nouns (section 3.2) in exactly the same fashion.

DIvI'may'DujmeyDaq *at/to the Federation battle cruisers*

DIvI'may'Duj	(noun)	*Federation battle cruiser*
-mey	(2)	*plural*
-Daq	(5)	*locative*

baHwI'pu'vam *these gunners*

baHwI'	(noun)	*gunner*
-pu'	(2)	*plural*
-vam	(4)	*this*

3.4. The noun–noun construction

Some combinations of two (or more) nouns in a row are so common as to have become everyday words. These are the compound nouns (as discussed in section 3.2.1). In addition, it is possible to combine nouns in the manner of a compound noun to produce a new construct even if it is not a legitimate compound noun ("legitimate" in the sense that it would be found in a dictionary).

The translation of two nouns combined in this way, say

N1–N2 (that is, noun #1 followed by noun #2), would be *N2 of the N1*. For example, **nuH** *weapon* and **pegh** *secret* combine to form **nuH pegh** *secret of the weapon*. An alternate translation would be *N1's N2*, in this case, *the weapon's secret*. As discussed in section 3.3.4, this is the Klingon possessive construction for a noun possessed by another noun.

When the noun–noun construction is used, only the second noun can take syntactic suffixes (Type 5). Both nouns, however, may take suffixes of the other four types. For example:

nuHvam pegh *secret of this weapon*

nuH	(noun)	*weapon*
-vam	(4)	*this*
pegh	(noun)	*secret*

jaghpu' yuQmeyDaq *at/to the enemies' planets*

jagh	(noun)	*enemy*
-pu'	(2)	*plural*
yuQ	(noun)	*planet*
-mey	(2)	*plural*
-Daq	(5)	*locative*

puqwI' qamDu' *my child's feet*

puq	(noun)	*child*
-wI'	(4)	*my*
qam	(noun)	*foot*
-Du	(2)	*plural*

English prepositional phrases are also rendered in Klingon by this noun–noun construction. Prepositional concepts such as *above* and *below* are actually nouns in Klingon, best translated as "area above," "area below," etc. The locative suffix (section 3.3.5) follows the second noun. For example:

nagh DungDaq *above the rock*

nagh	(noun)	*rock*
Dung	(noun)	*area above*
-Daq	(5)	*locative*

More literally, this is "at the area above the rock" or "at the rock's above-area."

4. VERBS

Klingon verbs are mostly monosyllabic forms which may be accompanied by several affixes. As with Klingon nouns, Klingon verbs may take suffixes falling into a number of types based on their relative position following the verb. There are nine types of verb suffixes. Unlike Klingon nouns, Klingon verbs may take prefixes. Thus, if suffix types are indicated as numbers, the structure of a Klingon verb is:

PREFIX–VERB–1–2–3–4–5–6–7–8–9

4.1. Pronominal prefixes

Each Klingon verb begins with a single prefix that indicates who or what is performing the action described by the verb and, when relevant, who or what is the recipient of that action. In other words, Klingon verb prefixes indicate both the subject and the object of the sentence.

4.1.1. Basic prefixes

The basic set of prefixes can be presented in a chart. (In order to make the chart as clear as possible, some prefixes are repeated.)

Note that both the subject and the object are combined

VERBS

OBJECT / SUBJECT	none	*me*	*you*	*him/ her/it*	*us*	*you (plural)*	*them*
I	jI-	–	qa-	vI-	–	Sa-	vI-
you	bI-	cho-	–	Da-	ju-	–	Da-
he/she/it	0	mu-	Du-	0	nu-	lI-	0
we	ma-	–	pI-	wI-	–	re-	DI-
you (plural)	Su-	tu-	–	bo-	che-	–	bo-
they	0	mu-	nI-	lu-	nu-	lI-	0

into a single prefix. 0 in the chart means that the particular subject-object combinations are indicated by the absence of a prefix before the verb; – in the chart notes subject-object combinations which cannot be expressed with the Klingon verb prefix system. For such meanings, suffixes (section 4.2.1) and/or pronouns (section 5.1) must be used.

The prefixes in the first column of the chart (headed "none") are used when there is no object; that is, when the action of the verb affects only the subject (the "doer"). The verb **Qong** *sleep* occurs with the pronominal prefixes as follows:

> **jIQong** *I sleep*
> **bIQong** *you sleep*
> **Qong** *he/she/it sleeps, they sleep*
> **maQong** *we sleep*
> **SuQong** *you (plural) sleep*

In the case of **Qong** *he/she/it sleeps, they sleep,* the exact subject would be indicated elsewhere in the sentence or by context.

This set of prefixes is also used when an object is possible, but unknown or vague. Thus, **jIyaj** *I understand* can be used when the speaker understands things in general, knows what is going on, or understands what another speaker has just said. It cannot, however, be used for understanding a language or understanding a person. Similarly, **maSop** *we eat* can be used to indicate a general act of eating, but not if a specific food is mentioned.

The remaining prefixes combine subject and object. Some of them are illustrated below, using the verb **legh** *see*.

qalegh *I see you*

vIlegh *I see him/her/it/them*

Salegh *I see you (plural)*

cholegh *you see me*

mulegh *he/she/it sees me, they see me*

tulegh *you (plural) see me*

Dalegh *you see him/her/it/them*

julegh *you see us*

Dulegh *he/she/it sees you*

pIlegh *we see you*

legh *he/she/it sees him/her/it/them, they see them*

lulegh *they see him/her/it*

4.1.2 Imperative prefixes

A special set of prefixes is used for imperatives, that is, verbs giving commands. Commands can be given only to *you* or *you (plural)*.

OBJECT	none	*me*	*him/her/it*	*us*	*them*
you	**yI-**	**HI-**	**yI-**	**gho-**	**tI-**
you (plural)	**pe-**	**HI-**	**yI-**	**gho-**	**tI-**

Note that, with one exception, the identical prefix is used regardless of whether the command is being given to one or more than one person. The single exception is when a command is given but there is no object. In such cases, a special prefix **pe-** is used to give a command to several people. Examples of the imperative prefixes follow. Exclamation points in the translation indicate that it is a command.

yIQong *sleep!*

HIqIp *hit me!*

peQong *(you plural) sleep!*

ghoqIp *hit us!*

yIqIp *hit him/her/it!*   **tIqIp** *hit them!*

To indicate action directed against oneself in an imperative verb (e.g., *tell yourself*), the suffix **-egh** *oneself* is used along with **yI-** or **pe-** (see section 4.2.1).

4.1.3 Notational conventions

As a notational convention, prefixes indicating subject and object will be translated as *subject–object;* e.g., **qa-** *I–you*, **DI-** *we–them*. Imperative prefixes will be translated similarly, preceded by the word *imperative:* **tI-** *imperative: you–them*.

Also, prefixes which can refer to male, female, inanimate, singular, and/or plural (e.g., **vI-** *I–him/her/it/them*) will be translated correctly, but usually without giving all the options (e.g., *I–him/her*). This convention will also be used when translating verbs containing these prefixes; e.g., **vIlegh** *I see him/her*.

4.2. Verb suffixes

There are nine types of verb suffixes.

4.2.1. Type 1: Oneself/one another

-egh *oneself*

This suffix is used to indicate that the action described by the verb affects the performer of the action, the subject. It is translated by English *self*. When this suffix is used, the prefix set indicating "no object" must also be used.

> **jIqIp'egh** *I hit myself* (**qIp** *hit*)
> **bIqIp'egh** *you hit yourself*
> **qIp'egh** *he/she hits himself/herself*

It is also possible to use this suffix with imperative verbs. As with nonimperatives, the prefix indicating "no object" must be used.

> **yIja''egh** *tell yourself!* (**ja'** *tell*)
> **peja''egh** *tell yourselves!*

-chuq *one another*

This suffix is used only with plural subjects. It is translated *each other* or *one another*. The prefix set indicating "no object" is also used when this suffix is used.

> **maqIpchuq** *we hit each other* (**qIp** *hit*)
> **SuqIpchuq** *you (plural) hit each other*
> **qIpchuq** *they hit each other*
> **peqIpchuq** *hit each other!*

4.2.2. Type 2: Volition/predisposition

Suffixes of this type express how much choice the subject has about the action described or how predisposed the subject is to doing it.

-nIS *need*

> **vIleghnIS** *I need to see him/her* (**legh** *see*)
> **bISopnIS** *you need to eat* (**Sop** *eat*)

-qang *willing*

> **Heghqang** *he/she is willing to die* (**Hegh** *die*)
> **qaja'qang** *I am willing to tell you* (**ja'** *tell*)

-rup *ready, prepared* (referring to beings)

> **Heghrup** *he/she is ready to die* (**Hegh** *die*)
> **qaleghrup** *I am ready to see you* (**legh** *see*)
> **nuja'rup** *they are prepared to tell us* (**ja'** *tell*)

-beH *ready, set up* (referring to devices)

> **pojbeH** *(the device) is set up to analyze it* (**poj** *analyze*)
> **labbeH** *(the device) is ready to transmit data* (**lab**
> *transmit data*)

There is, it should be noted, a verb **ghuS** which means *to be prepared to launch or project (something)*. This verb never takes the suffix **-rup.** It is used primarily in reference to torpedoes—so much so that if the object is not specifically stated, and context does not dictate otherwise, it is always assumed to be *torpedoes*. Accordingly, both of the following sentences mean *Be prepared to launch torpedoes!* or *Stand by on torpedoes!*

> **cha yIghuS**   (**cha** *torpedoes*)
> **yIghuS**

The verb **ghuS** can also be used in reference to, among other things, rockets, missiles, and various kinds of energy beams (which, like torpedoes, go from one point to another). It is also used to describe the action of pulling back the elastic band of a slingshot. In most other instances of preparedness, however, **-rup** is required.

-vIp *afraid*

choHoHvIp *you are afraid to kill me* (**HoH** *kill*)
nuqIpvIp *they are afraid to hit us* (**qIp** *hit*)

This suffix is rarely used with a prefix meaning *I* or *we*. Though it is grammatically correct, it is culturally taboo.

4.2.3. Type 3: Change

Suffixes of this type indicate that the action described by the verb involves a change of some kind from the state of affairs that existed before the action took place.

-choH *change in state, change in direction*

maDo'choH *we are becoming lucky, we are undergoing a turn of luck* (**Do'** *be lucky*)
ghoSchoH *he/she is beginning to go (somewhere)* (**ghoS** *go*)

The implication of the second example is that he or she was going either nowhere or somewhere else sometime before the phrase was uttered. Note that the translation of this suffix may be English *become* or *begin to*.

-qa' *resume*

Using this suffix implies that an action had been taking place, then it stopped, and then it began again.

vInejqa' *I am resuming the search, I am searching for*

him/her again (**nej** *search*)

4.2.4. Type 4: Cause

-moH *cause*

Adding this suffix to a verb indicates that the subject is causing a change of condition or causing a new condition to come into existence.

> **tIjwI'ghom vIchenmoH** *I form a boarding party*
> (**tIjwI'ghom** *boarding party,*
> **chen** *take form, take shape*)

This sentence might also be translated *I cause a boarding party to be formed.*

> **HIQoymoH** *let me hear (something)* (**Qoy** *hear*)

More revealingly, this sentence could be translated *cause me to hear (something).* Note that this sentence would not be used in asking permission to hear; it is a direct command.

Normally, the best English translation of a verb with **-moH** does not contain the word *cause.* For example, **chenmoH** *he/she makes, creates* could be translated *he/she causes to take shape* (**chen** *take form, take shape*), but this is an awkward English phrase.

4.2.5. Type 5: Indefinite subject/ability

The two suffixes of Type 5 have nothing much to do with each other except for both being Type 5. As a result, no verb occurs with both of these suffixes at the same time.

-lu' *indefinite subject*

This suffix is used to indicate that the subject is unknown, indefinite, and/or general. Since the subject is always the same (that is, it is always unstated), the pronominal prefixes (section 4.1.1) are used in a different way. Those prefixes which normally indicate first- or second-person subject and third-person singular object (**vI-**, **Da-**, **wI-**, **bo-**) are used to indicate first- or second-person object. Thus, **vI-**, which normally means *I do something to him/her*, when in a verb with **lu'** means *someone/something does something to me*. Similarly, the prefix **lu-**, which normally means *they do something to him/her*, becomes *someone/something does something to them*.

> **Daqawlu'** *someone/something remembers you*
>   (**qaw** *remember*)
> **wIleghlu'** *someone/something sees us* (**legh** *see*)
> **Soplu'** *someone/something eats it* (**Sop** *eat*)

Verbs with **-lu'** are often translated into the English passive voice.

> **Daqawlu'** *you are remembered*
> **wIleghlu'** *we are seen*
> **Soplu'** *it is eaten*

When used with the verb **tu'** *find, observe* and a third-person singular subject pronoun (0), the resulting verb form **tu'lu'** *someone/something finds it* is often translated by English *there is*.

> **naDev puqpu' tu'lu'** *there are children around here, someone/something finds children here* (**naDev** *hereabouts*, **puqpu'** *children*)

-laH *can, able*

> **jIQonglaH** *I can sleep* (**Qong** *sleep*)
> **choleghlaH** *you can see me* (**legh** *see*)
> **nuQaw'laH** *he/she can destroy us* (**Qaw'** *destroy*)

4.2.6. Type 6: Qualification

Like Type 3 noun suffixes, these suffixes show how sure the speaker is about what is being said.

-chu' *clearly, perfectly*

jIyajchu' *I understand clearly* (**yaj** *understand*)
baHchu' *he/she fired (the torpedo) perfectly* (**baH** *fire [a torpedo]*)

-bej *certainly, undoubtedly*

chImbej *it is undoubtedly empty* (**chIm** *be empty*)
nuSeHbej *he/she is certainly controlling us* (**SeH** *control*)

-law' *seemingly, apparently*

chImlaw' *it appears to be empty* (**chIm** *be empty*)
nuSeHlaw' *he/she seems to be controlling us* (**SeH** *control*)

This suffix expresses any uncertainty on the speaker's part and may even be thought of as meaning *I think* or *I suspect*. Thus, the previous two sentences could be translated *I think it's empty, I suspect that he/she is controlling us.*

4.2.7. Type 7: Aspect

Klingon does not express tenses (past, present, future). These ideas come across from context or other words in the sentence (such as **wa'leS** *tomorrow*). The language does, however, indicate aspect: whether an action is completed or not yet completed, and whether an action is a single event or a continuing one.

The absence of a Type 7 suffix usually means that the action is not completed and is not continuous (that is, it is not one of the things indicated by the Type 7 suffixes). Verbs with no Type 7 suffix are translated by the English simple present tense.

> **Dalegh** *you see him/her* (**legh** *see*)
> **qaja'** *I tell you* (**ja'** *tell*)

When the context is appropriate, verbs without a Type 7 suffix may be translated by the English future tense *(will)*, but the real feeling of the Klingon is closer to English sentences such as *We fly tomorrow at dawn*, where the present-tense verb refers to an event in the future.

VERBS

-pu' *perfective*

This suffix indicates that an action is completed. It is often translated by the English present perfect *(have done something)*.

> **Daleghpu'** *you have seen it* (**legh** *see*)
> **vIneHpu'** *I wanted them* (**neH** *want*)
> **qaja'pu'** *I told you* (**ja'** *tell*)

-ta' *accomplished, done*

This suffix is similar to **-pu'**, but it is used when an activity was deliberately undertaken, the implication being that someone set out to do something and in fact did it. English translations seldom reveal the distinction.

> **vISuqta'** *I have acquired it* (**Suq** *get, acquire*)
> **luHoHta'** *they have killed him/her* (**HoH** *kill*)

The second sentence above could not be used if the killing were the result of a general attack not intended to kill a specific person or if the killing were an accident. In such cases, **-pu'** would be used:

> **luHoHpu'** *they have killed him/her*

The meaning of **-ta'** can also be indicated syntactically. That is, instead of using the suffix **-ta'**, a special verbal construction can follow the verb which indicates the accomplished action. This special verb is **rIn** *be finished, accomplished*, and in this usage it always takes the suffix **-taH** *continuous* (see below) and the third-person pronominal prefix (0). The resulting construction, **rIntaH,** literally means *it continues to be finished* or *it remains accomplished*. It is used to indicate that the action denoted by the preceding verb is a fait accompli: it is done, and it cannot be undone.

> **luHoH rIntaH** *they have killed him/her* (**HoH** *kill*)
> **vIje' rIntaH** *I have purchased it* (**je'** *purchase*)

The English translations of **rIntaH** and **-ta'** are usually the same. The notion of absolute finality implied by **rIntaH** seldom comes across.

It should be noted that **rIntaH** is sometimes used for

dramatic effect, even in cases when the action could be undone.

-taH *continuous*

This suffix indicates that an action is ongoing.

> **nughoStaH** *it is approaching us* (**ghoS** *approach*)
> **yIghoStaH** *steady on course!, maintain this course!*
> (**ghoS** *go, approach, proceed on a course*)

Both of the above sentences suggest a continuing activity. The meaning of **-taH** can be seen clearly by comparing the following two commands:

> **yIjun** *execute an evasive maneuver!*
> **yIjuntaH** *take evasive action!*

In the first case, the maneuver is to be executed once only. In the second, a series of evasive maneuvers is to be executed —the action is to be continuous.

-lI' *in progress*

This suffix is similar to **-taH** *continuous* in that it indicates that an activity is ongoing. Unlike **-taH,** however, **-lI'** implies that the activity has a known goal or a definite stopping point. In other words, it suggests that progress is being made toward that goal.

> **chollI'** *it is getting closer*
> (**chol** *get close, come near*)

This word would be used for, i.e., a missile approaching a target, when it is known that the missile has been aimed at that target. If a missile is getting closer, but its intended destination is not known, **choltaH** (with **-taH** *continuous*) would be more appropriate.

> **vIlI'lI'** *I am transmitting (the data)*
> (**lI'** *transmit data to a place*)

This word implies that data are in the process of being transmitted, but that there is a finite amount of data, so there will be a definite end to the transmission. The fact that the verb **lI'** and the suffix **-lI'** are identical in sound is purely coincidental, so far as can be determined.

The suffix **-taH** *continuous* can be used whether there is a known goal or not. **-ll'**, on the other hand, can be used only when there is an implied goal. It is possible to consider **-ll'** a *continuous* counterpart of **-ta'**, and **-taH** a *continuous* counterpart of **-pu'**.

4.2.8. Type 8: Honorific

-neS *honorific*

There is but one suffix in this category. It is used to express extreme politeness or deference. It is used only in addressing a superior, someone of higher rank in the Klingon social, political, or military hierarchy. It is never required.

> **qaleghneS** *I am honored to see you* (**legh** *see*)
> **HIja'neS** *do me the honor of telling me* (**ja'** *tell*)

This suffix is used rather infrequently by Klingons.

4.2.9. Type 9: Syntactic markers

Similar to Type 5 noun suffixes (section 3.3.5), these verb suffixes have to do with the verb's role in the sentence. The first six suffixes will be noted briefly here, but illustrated more completely in section 6.2.

-DI' *as soon as, when*

> **DaSeHDI'** *as soon as you control it* (**SeH** *control*)
> **qara'DI'** *as soon as I command you* (**ra'** *command*)

-chugh *if*

> **DaneHchugh** *if you want them* (**neH** *want*)
> **choja'chugh** *if you tell me* (**ja'** *tell*)

-pa' *before*

> **choja'pa'** *before you tell me* (**ja'** *tell*)
> **qara'pa'** *before I command you* (**ra'** *command*)

-vIS *while*

This suffix is always used along with the Type 7 suffix

-taH *continuous.*

SutlhtaHvIS *while they are negotiating* (**Sutlh** *negotiate*)
bIQongtaHvIS *while you are sleeping* (**Qong** *sleep*)

-bogh *which*

This is the relative-clause marker. It is described in section 6.2.3.

-meH *for*

This marks purpose clauses. See section 6.2.4.

-'a' *interrogative*

This suffix indicates that the sentence is a yes/no question; that is, a question which can be answered "yes" or "no." (See also section 6.4.).

> **cholegh'a'** *do you see me?* (**legh** *see*)
> **yaj'a'** *does he/she understand?* (**yaj** *understand*)

Questions of other types require special question words (section 6.4).

-wI' *one who does, thing which does*

This is the suffix described earlier (section 3.2.2) which turns verbs into nouns.

> **So'wI'** *cloaking device* (**So'** *cloak, hide*)
> **baHwI'** *gunner* (**baH** *fire* [*a torpedo*])
> **joqwI'** *flag* (**joq** *flutter, wave*)

4.2.10. Relative ordering of the suffixes

As with nouns, when more than one suffix is used with a verb, they must occur in the correct order, according to their type. No more than one suffix of each type may occur at a time. No instances have been found of a verb followed by nine suffixes, but it is theoretically possible. A few examples should suffice to show ordering of the suffixes.

> **nuHotlhpu''a'** *have they scanned us?*
> **nu-**   (prefix)   *they–us*
> **Hotlh**   (verb)   *scan*

| -pu' | (7) | *perfective* |
| -'a' | (9) | *interrogative* |

Qaw''eghpu' *he/she destroyed himself/herself*

0	(prefix)	*he/she*
Qaw'	(verb)	*destroy*
-'egh	(1)	*oneself*
-pu'	(7)	*perfective*

wIchenmoHlaH *we can create it*

wI-	(prefix)	*we-it*
chen	(verb)	*take form*
-moH	(4)	*cause*
-laH	(5)	*can, able*

Daqawlu'taH *you are to be remembered*

Da-	(prefix)	*you–him/her*
qaw	(verb)	*remember*
-lu'	(5)	*indefinite subject*
-taH	(7)	*continuous*

vItlhapnISpu' *I needed to take him/her*

vI-	(prefix)	*I–him/her*
tlhap	(verb)	*take*
-nIS	(2)	*need*
-pu'	(7)	*perfective*

HeghqangmoHlu'pu' *it made him/her willing to die*

0	(prefix)	*he/she–him/her*
Hegh	(verb)	*die*
-qang	(2)	*willing*
-moH	(4)	*cause*
-lu'	(5)	*indefinite subject*
-pu'	(7)	*perfective*

maghoSchoHmoHneS'a' *may we execute a course (to some place)?*

ma-	(prefix)	*we*
ghoS	(verb)	*proceed on a course*
-choH	(3)	*change*
-moH	(4)	*cause*
-neS	(8)	*honorific*
-'a'	(9)	*interrogative*

4.3. Rovers

There is one additional set of verb suffixes which Klingon grammarians call **lengwI'mey** *rovers* (from **leng** *travel, roam, rove,* **-wI'** *thing which does,* **-mey** *plural*). Rovers are verb suffixes which do not have a fixed position in relation to the other suffixes following a verb but, instead, can come just about anywhere except following a Type 9 suffix. Their position is determined by the meaning intended. There are two types of rovers: the negative and the emphatic.

-be' *not*

This is the general suffix of negation, translated as English *not*. It follows the concept being negated.

vIlo'laHbe' *they are useless to me, I cannot use them*

vI-	(prefix)	*I—them*
lo'	(verb)	*use*
-laH	(5)	*can, able*
-be'	(rover)	*not*

jISaHbe' *I don't care (which of several courses of action is followed)*

jI-	(prefix)	*I*
SaH	(verb)	*care, be concerned about*
-be'	(rover)	*not*

qay'be' *it's not a problem, no problem (exclamation)*

0	(prefix)	*it*
qay'	(verb)	*be a problem, be a hassle*
-be'	(rover)	*not*

The roving nature of **-be'** is best illustrated in the following set of words.

choHoHvIp *you are afraid to kill me*
choHoHvIpbe' *you are not afraid to kill me*
choHoHbe'vIp *you are afraid to not kill me*

cho-	(prefix)	*you—me*
HoH	(verb)	*kill*
-vIp	(2)	*afraid*
-be'	(rover)	*not*

In the second word, the negated notion is *afraid* (that is, *not afraid*), and **-be'** follows **-vIp**. In the third word, the negated notion is *kill* (that is, *not kill*), so **-be'** follows **HoH**.

VERBS

The suffix **-be'** cannot be used with imperative verbs. For imperatives, the following suffix is required.

-Qo' *don't!, won't*

This negative suffix is used in imperatives and to denote refusal.

> **yIja'Qo'** *don't tell him/her!*
>
> | | | |
> |---|---|---|
> | **yI-** | (prefix) | *imperative: you–him/her* |
> | **ja'** | (verb) | *tell* |
> | **-Qo'** | (rover) | *don't!* |

> **choja'Qo'chugh** *if you won't tell me, if you refuse to tell me*
>
> | | | |
> |---|---|---|
> | **cho-** | (prefix) | *you–me* |
> | **ja'** | (verb) | *tell* |
> | **-Qo'** | (rover) | *won't* |
> | **-chugh** | (9) | *if* |

> **HIHoHvIpQo'** *don't be afraid to kill me!*
>
> | | | |
> |---|---|---|
> | **HI-** | (prefix) | *imperative: you–me* |
> | **HoH** | (verb) | *kill* |
> | **-vIp** | (2) | *afraid* |
> | **-Qo'** | (rover) | *don't!* |

Unlike **-be'**, the position of **-Qo'** does not change: it occurs last, unless followed by a Type 9 suffix. Nevertheless, it is considered a rover because it is the imperative counterpart to **-be'**.

-Ha' *undo*

This negative suffix implies not merely that something is not done (as does **-be'**), but that there is a change of state: something that was previously done is now undone. For convenience, it will here be translated as *undo*, but it is closer to the English prefixes *mis-, de-, dis-* (as in *misunderstand, demystify, disentangle*). It is also used if something is done wrongly. Unlike **-be'**, **-Ha'** can be used in imperatives.

> **chenHa'moHlaH** *it can destroy them*
>
> | | | |
> |---|---|---|
> | 0 | (prefix) | *it–them* |
> | **chen** | (verb) | *take form* |

47

-Ha'	(rover)	*undo*
-moH	(4)	*cause*
-laH	(5)	*can, able*

This verb actually means something like *it can cause them to undo their form.*

yIchu'Ha' *disengage it! (e.g., cloaking device)*

yI-	(prefix)	*imperative: you–it*
chu'	(verb)	*engage, activate*
-Ha'	(rover)	*undo*

bIjatlhHa'chugh *if you say the wrong thing*

bI-	(prefix)	*you*
jatlh	(verb)	*say*
-Ha'	(rover)	*undo*
-chugh	(9)	*if*

This shows how **-Ha'** can be used in the sense of *wrongly*. The word might be translated as *if you misspeak*. Using **-be'** (that is, **bIjatlhbe'chugh**) would mean *if you don't speak*.

Do'Ha' *it is unfortunate*

0	(prefix)	*it*
-Do'	(verb)	*be lucky, fortunate*
-Ha'	(rover)	*undo*

The use of **-Ha'** in this sentence suggests a turn of luck from good to bad.

It is interesting that **-Ha'** always occurs right after the verb. It is not known why Klingon grammarians insist on calling it a rover. It was felt best not to argue with Klingon tradition, however, so **-Ha'** is here classified as a rover.

-qu' *emphatic*

This suffix emphasizes or affirms whatever immediately precedes it.

yIHaghqu' *study him/her well*

yI-	(prefix)	*imperative: you–him/her*
Hagh	(verb)	*study*
-qu'	(rover)	*emphatic*

nuQaw'qu'be' *they have not finished us off*

nu-	(prefix)	*they–us*

Qaw'	(verb)	*destroy*
-qu'	(rover)	*emphatic*
-be'	(rover)	*not*

The roving nature of **-qu'** can be seen in the following set:

pIHoHvIpbe'qu' *we are NOT afraid to kill you*
pIHoHvIpqu'be' *we are not AFRAID to kill you*
pIHoHqu'vIpbe' *we are not afraid to KILL you*

pI-	(prefix)	*we–you*
HoH	(verb)	*kill*
-vIp	(2)	*afraid*
-be'	(rover)	*not*
-qu'	(rover)	*emphatic*

The first word above might be used after an enemy challenged the bravery of the speaker. The second might be followed by an explanation such as, "We are not willing to kill you because we require your services." The third word would be used to emphasize killing, as opposed to some other form of punishment.

The rover **-qu'** also follows verbs when they are used adjectivally (section 4.4).

4.4 Adjectives

There are no adjectives as such in Klingon. Those notions expressed as adjectives in English (such as *big, tired*) are expressed by verbs in Klingon *(be big, be tired)*. A verb expressing a state or quality can be used immediately following a noun to modify that noun.

puq Doy' *tired child*
puq *child*
Doy' *be tired*

Dujmey tIn *big ships*
Dujmey *ships, vessels*
tIn *be big*

The rover **-qu'** *emphatic* (section 4.3) may follow verbs functioning adjectivally. In this usage, it is usually translated *very*.

Dujmey tInqu' *very big ships*

wanI' ramqu' *a very unimportant event*
wanI' *event, occurrence*
ram *be trivial, unimportant*

If a Type 5 noun suffix is used (section 3.3.5), it follows the verb, which, when used to modify the noun in this way, can have no other suffix except the rover **-qu'** *emphatic*. The Type 5 noun suffix follows **-qu'**.

veng tInDaq *in the big city*
veng *city*
tIn *be big*
-Daq *locative*

veng tInqu'Daq *in the very big city*

5. OTHER KINDS OF WORDS

By far the bulk of Klingon words are nouns and verbs. There are a few others which, probably as an expedient, Klingon grammarians lump together in a group called **chuvmey** *leftovers*. It is possible to classify the **chuvmey** somewhat.

5.1. Pronouns

In addition to possessive suffixes for nouns (section 3.3.4) and pronominal prefixes for verbs (section 4.1), there is a set of nine pronouns which are independent words.

jIH *I, me*	**maH** *we, us*
soH *you*	**tlhIH** *you (plural)*
ghaH *he/she, him/her*	**chaH** *they, them*
'oH *it*	**bIH** *they, them*
'e' *that*	
net *that*	

The pronoun **chaH** *they* is used when it refers to a group of beings capable of using language; otherwise, **bIH** *they* is used. The pronouns **'e'** and **net** are used only in special sentence constructions (see section 6.2.5).

There is no grammatical gender in Klingon. Third-person

51

singular pronouns can be translated *he* or *she* as context dictates.

Pronouns may be used as nouns, but only for emphasis or added clarity. They are not required. Thus, the following sets of sentences are all grammatically correct.

yaS vIlegh jIH **yaS vIlegh**	*I see the officers.*
jIH mulegh yaS **mulegh yaS**	*The officer sees me.*
ghaH vIlegh jIH **ghaH vIlegh** **vIlegh jIH** **vIlegh**	*I see him/her.*

(**yaS** *officer,* **vIlegh** *I see him/her,* **mulegh** *he/she sees me*)

The final two sentences (**vIlegh jIH, vIlegh**) are in fact ambiguous. They could equally well mean *I see them.* (The verb prefix **vI-** is either *I–him/her* or *I–them.*) If context does not make it clear which meaning is intended, pronouns can be used:

> **ghaH vIlegh** *I see him/her.*
> **chaH vIlegh** *I see them.*

Pronouns are not used in possessive constructions in the way nouns are; instead, the set of possessive noun suffixes is used (section 3.3.4).

Finally, pronouns can be used as verbs, in the sense of "I am," etc. (See section 6.3.)

5.2. Numbers

Klingon originally had a ternary number system; that is, one based on three. Counting proceeded as follows: 1, 2, 3; 3+1, 3+2, 3+3; 2×3+1, 2×3+2, 2×3+3; 3×3+1, 3×3+2, 3×3+3; and then it got complicated. In accordance with the more accepted practice, the Klingon Empire sometime back adopted a decimal number system, one based on ten.

OTHER KINDS OF WORDS

Though no one knows for sure, it is likely that this change was made more out of concern for understanding the scientific data of other civilizations than out of a spirit of cooperation.

The Klingon numbers are:

1	wa'	6	jav
2	cha'	7	Soch
3	wej	8	chorgh
4	loS	9	Hut
5	vagh	10	wa'maH

Higher numbers are formed by adding special number-forming elements to the basic set of numbers (1–9). Thus, **wa'maH** *ten* consists of **wa'** *one* plus the number-forming element for *ten,* **maH.** Counting continues as follows:

11	**wa'maH wa'**	(that is, *ten and one*)
12	**wa'maH cha'**	(that is, *ten and two*)
etc.		

Higher numbers are based on **maH** *ten,* **vatlh** *hundred,* and **SaD** or **SanID** *thousand.* Both **SaD** and **SanID** are equally correct for *thousand,* and both are used with roughly equal frequency. It is not known why this number alone has two variants.

20	**cha'maH**	(that is, *two tens*)
30	**wejmaH**	(that is, *three tens*)
etc.		

100	**wa'vatlh**	(that is, *one hundred*)
200	**cha'vatlh**	(that is, *two hundreds*)
etc.		

1,000	**wa'SaD** or **wa'SanID**	(that is, *one thousand*)
2,000	**cha'SaD** or **cha'SanID**	(that is, *two thousands*)
etc.		

Numbers are combined as in English:

5,347 **vaghSad wejvatlh loSmaH Soch** or

53

vaghSanID wejvatlh loSmaH Soch
    604 **javvatlh loS**
    31 **wejmaH wa'**

Some of the number-forming elements for higher numbers are:

ten thousand	**netlh**
hundred thousand	**bIp**
million	**'uy'**

Zero is **pagh.**

Numbers are used as nouns. As such, they may stand alone as subjects or objects or they may modify another noun.

> **mulegh cha'** *Two (of them) see me.*
>   (**mulegh** *they see me,* **cha'** *two*)

> **wa' yIHoH** *Kill one (of them)!*
>   (**wa'** *one,* **yIHoH** *kill him/her!*)

The preceding sentence is grammatically correct even without the **wa'** because the prefix **yI-** indicates a singular object. The **wa',** therefore, is used for emphasis only.

Numbers used as modifiers precede the noun they modify.

> **loS puqpu'** or **loS puq** *four children*
> **vaghmaH yuQmey** or **vaghmaH yuQ** *fifty planets*

The plural suffixes (**-pu', -mey**) are not necessary when a number is used.

When a number is used for numbering, as opposed to counting, it follows the noun. Compare:

> **DuS wa'** *torpedo tube number 1*
> **wa' DuS** *one torpedo tube*

Ordinal numbers (*first, second,* etc.) are formed by adding **-DIch** to the numbers.

> **wa'DIch** *first*
> **cha'DIch** *second*
> **HutDIch** *ninth*

Ordinal numbers follow the noun.

> **meb cha'DIch** *second guest*

Adding **-logh** to a number gives the notion of repetitions.

> **wa'logh** *once*
> **cha'logh** *twice*
> **Hutlogh** *nine times*

These numbers function in the sentence as adverbials (section 5.4).

5.3. Conjunctions

Conjunctions are of two types: those that join nouns together and those that join sentences together. The meanings of the two types of conjunctions, however, are the same:

JOINING NOUNS	JOINING SENTENCES	
je	**'ej**	*and*
joq	**qoj**	*and/or*
ghap	**pagh**	*either/or*

The conjunctions joining nouns come after the final noun.

> **DeS 'uS je** *an arm and a leg*
> **DeS 'uS joq** *an arm or a leg or both*
> **DeS 'uS ghap** *either an arm or a leg (but not both)*

The noun conjunction **je** has an additional function: when it follows a verb, it means *also, too.*

> **qaleghpu' je** *I also saw you, I saw you too*

As in English, the meaning of such sentences is ambiguous: *I and others saw you* or *I saw you and others.* The exact meaning is determined by context.

In addition to the three listed above, there is one other sentence conjunction:

> **'ach** *but, nevertheless, however, even so*

This word is sometimes shortened to **'a.**

The conjunctions joining sentences occur between the sentences they join. For illustrations, see section 6.2.1.

5.4. Adverbials

These words usually come at the beginning of a sentence and describe the manner of the activity.

batlh *with honor, in an honored fashion*
bong *by accident, accidentally, not intentionally*
chaq *perhaps*
chIch *on purpose, purposely*
DaH *now*
Do' *with luck, luckily*
loQ *slightly, a little bit*
nom *fast, quickly*
not *never*
pay' *suddenly*
pIj *often*
QIt *slowly*
reH *always*
rut *sometimes*
tugh *soon*
vaj *thus, in that case, so, accordingly, then*
wej *not yet*

Examples:

bong yaS vIHoHpu' *I accidentally killed the officer.*
(**yaS** *officer,* **vIHoHpu'** *I killed him/her*)
batlh Daqawlu'taH *You will be remembered with honor.*
(**Daqawlu'taH** *somebody continues to remember you*)
vaj Daleghpu' *Then you have seen it.*
(**Daleghpu'** *you have seen it*)
wej vIlegh *I don't see him/her yet*
(**vIlegh** *I see him/her*)

One word fits somewhat awkwardly into this category:

neH *only, merely, just*

Unlike the other adverbials, it follows the verb which it modifies. The semantic effect is one of trivializing the action.

qama' vIqIppu' neH *I merely hit the prisoner.*
(**qama'** *prisoner,* **vIqIppu'** *I hit him/her*)
Duj yIQotlh neH *Just disable the ship!*
(**Duj** *ship, vessel,* **yIQotlh** *disable it!*)

56

The use of **neH** in the preceding sentence implies that the ship is to be disabled, but not damaged further.

Also unlike the other adverbials, **neH** can follow a noun. In such cases, it means *only, alone*.

> **yaS neH** *only the officer, the officer alone*
> **jonta' neH** *only the engine*

Adverbials sometimes occur alone, functioning more or less as exclamations (section 5.5). For example:

> **nom** *Move fast! Move quickly!*
> **wej** *Don't do it yet!*
> **tugh** *Hurry up!*

5.5 Exclamations

These expressions stand as sentences in their own right.

> **ghobe'** *No.* (response to a question)
> **Ha'** *Let's go! Come on!*
> **HIja'** or **HISlaH** *Yes.* (response to a question)
> **lu'** or **luq** *Yes. Okay. I will.*
> **maj** *Good.* (expressing satisfaction)
> **majQa'** *Very good. Well done.*
> **nuqneH** *What do you want?* (greeting)
> **pItlh** *Done!*
> **Qo'** *No. I won't. I refuse.*
> **SuH** or **Su'** *Ready!*
> **toH** *Well! So!*
> **wejpuH** *Charming.* (used only ironically)
> **'eH** *Ready!*

HIja' and **HISlaH** *yes* seem to be used interchangeably.

SuH, Su', and **'eH** all mean that the speaker is about to give a command. They are comparable to the "Ready!" at the beginning of a race: "Ready! Set! Go!" **SuH** and **Su'**, but not **'eH**, can also be used to indicate that the speaker is ready to do something or that arrangements have been made for something to happen. Some speakers of Klingon pronounce **SuH** as if it were **SSS**, almost like the English expression for "be quiet": *shhh!*

pItlh is used for *It's done! I've done it! I've finished! All done!* etc.

The expression **toH** is roughly equivalent to English *aha!*

Also included in the category of exclamations are Klingon curses. Only three such curses have been noted to date.

QI'yaH **?!#@*
ghuy'cha' **@$%*
Qu'vatlh *#*@!*

5.6. Names and address

Klingon names are frequently mispronounced by non-Klingons. Furthermore, when written in the writing systems of other languages, they usually end up with spellings which only suggest their true pronunciation. For example, the Klingon sound **tlh** at the beginning of a word is almost always written *kl* by English speakers, presumably because the sound *tl* cannot occur at the beginning of an English word. Similarly, Klingon **Q** is often rendered *kr,* and Klingon **q** always comes out *k.*

The following is a list of a few Klingon names along with their usual English spellings.

mara	*Mara*
matlh	*Maltz*
qeng	*Kang*
qeylIS	*Kahless*
qolotlh	*Koloth*
qor	*Kor*
qoreQ	*Korax*
QaS	*Kras*
Qel	*Krell*
Qugh	*Kruge*
torgh	*Torg*
valQIS	*Valkris*

Names may be used in direct address (that is, calling somebody by name) at the beginning or end of the sentence. Other words in direct address (such as **qaH** *sir,* **joHwI'** *my lord*) are used similarly.

> **torgh HIghoS** *Torg, come here!* (**HIghoS** *proceed toward me!*)
>
> **lu' qaH** *Yes, sir!*

6. SYNTAX

As in any language, Klingon sentences range from the very simple and straightforward to the very complex and convoluted. What follows here are the mere basics of Klingon sentence structure. This information should provide a good foundation so that students of Klingon can converse properly, though not eloquently, while learning more about the language.

6.1. Basic sentences

The basic structure of a Klingon sentence is:

OBJECT–VERB–SUBJECT

This is the reverse of the order in English, so care should be taken to avoid interpreting sentences backward. The subject is the person or thing doing the action described by the verb; the object is the recipient of that action.

The importance of word order can be seen by comparing the following sentences.

> **puq legh yaS** *The officer sees the child.*
> **yaS legh puq** *The child sees the officer.*

In both sentences, the words are identical: **puq** *child*, **legh** *he/she sees him/her,* **yaS** *officer.* The only way to know who is seeing whom is by the order of the words in the sentence. The verb **legh** is preceded by the prefix 0 *he/she–him/her.*

When the subject and/or object is first or second person, the prefix on the verb must be the proper one.

> **puq vIlegh jIH** *I see the child.*
> > (**vIlegh** *I see him/her*)
> **jIH mulegh puq** *The child sees me.*
> > (**mulegh** *he/she sees me*)

Actually, the first- and second-person pronouns are seldom used in sentences of this type (though they can, as here, be used for emphasis), so the following sentences illustrate more commonly occurring sentence types.

> **puq vIlegh** *I see the child.*
> **mulegh puq** *The child sees me.*

Imperative sentences (commands) follow the same rules.

> **So'wI' yIchu'** *Engage the cloaking device!*
> > (**So'wI'** *cloaking device,*
> > **yIchu'** *engage it!*)
> **DoS yIbuS** *Concentrate on the target!*
> > (**DoS** *target,* **yIbuS** *concentrate on it!*)
> **yaSpu' tIHoH** *Kill the officers!*
> > (**yaSpu'** *officers,* **tIHoH** *kill them!*)

Any noun in the sentence indicating something other than subject or object comes first, before the object noun. Such nouns usually end in a Type 5 noun suffix (section 3.3.5).

> **pa'Daq yaS vIleghpu'** *I saw the officer in the room.*
> > (**pa'Daq** *in the room,*
> > **yaS** *officer,* **vIleghpu'** *I saw him/her*)

Other examples of this construction are given in section 3.3.5.

6.2. Complex sentences

A few of the more common types of more elaborate Klingon sentences will be illustrated.

6.2.1. Compound sentences

Two sentences may be joined together to form a longer compound sentence. Both sentences must be able to stand alone as properly formed sentences. When combined, they simply come one after the other, joined by a conjunction (see section 5.3).

jISoptaH 'ej QongtaH *I am eating, and he/she is sleeping.*

jISoptaH 'ach QongtaH *I am eating, but he/she is sleeping.*

bISoptaH qoj bItlhutlhtaH *You are eating and/or you are drinking.*

bISoptaH pagh bItlhutlhtaH *You are either eating or else you are drinking.*

When the subject of both of the joined sentences is the same, the English translation may be reduced to a less choppy form, but Klingon does not allow this shortening. The pronominal prefix must be used with both verbs. Thus, the final two sentences above may be translated *You are eating and/or drinking; You are either eating or drinking.*

When a noun (as opposed to simply a verbal prefix) indicates subject and/or object, there are some options in Klingon. In its fullest form, a Klingon sentence repeats the noun:

> **yaS legh puq 'ej yaS qIp puq**
> (**yaS** *officer,* **puq** *child,* **legh** *he/she sees him/her,* **qIp** *he/she hits him/her*)
> *The child sees the officer and the child hits the officer.*
>
> or
>
> *The child sees the officer and hits the officer.*
>
> or
>
> *The child sees and hits the officer.*

It is possible, however, to use pronouns rather than nouns in the second of the joined sentences.

> **yaS legh puq 'ej ghaH qIp ghaH** (ghaH *he/she*)
> *The child sees the officer and he/she hits him/her.*
>
> or
>
> *The child sees the officer and hits him/her.*

If the context is clear, even the pronoun may be left out.

> **yaS vIlegh 'ej vIqIp** (vI- *I–him/her*)
> *I see the officer and I hit him/her.*
>
> or
>
> *I see the officer and hit him/her.*
>
> or
>
> *I see and hit the officer.*

6.2.2. Subordinate clauses

Klingon verbs ending in Type 9 suffixes (other than **-'a'** *interrogative* and **-wI'** *one who does, one which does*) always occur in sentences with another verb. Hence, they are verbs in subordinate clauses.

> **cha yIbaH qara'DI'**
> or **qara'DI' cha yIbaH** *Fire the torpedoes at my command!*

The two parts of this sentence are **cha yIbaH** *fire the torpedoes!* and **qara'DI'** *when I command you* or *as soon as I command you.* **-DI'** is a Type 9 suffix meaning *as soon as, when,* so **qara'DI'** must occur as part of a larger sentence. Note that the order of the two parts of the sentence is variable.

A few further examples should make the use of subordinate clauses clear.

> **bIjatlhHa'chugh qaHoH**
> or **qaHoH bIjatlhHa'chugh** *If you say the wrong thing, I will kill you.*
> (**bIjatlhHa'chugh** *if you misspeak,* **qaHoH** *I kill you*)

Note that although the English translation uses the word *will,* there is no marker for future in Klingon. The unsuffixed verb **HoH** *kill* is neutral as to time: since the person being addressed is being given a chance to speak, that person must still be alive. Thus, the killing must take place in the future.

SutlhtaHvIS chaH DIHIvpu'
or **DIHIvpu' SutlhtaHvIS chaH** *While they were*
negotiating we
attacked them.
(**SutlhtaHvIS** *while*
they are negotiating,
chaH *they,* **DIHIvpu'**
we attacked them)

The notion of *were negotiating,* rather than *are negotiating,* comes from the suffix **-pu'** *perfective* attached to the verb **HIv** *attack*. A translation such as *While they are negotiating we attacked them* makes little sense in English and misrepresents the meaning of the Klingon sentence.

6.2.3. Relative clauses

Relative clauses are translated into English as phrases beginning with *who, which, where,* and, most commonly, *that*. Like adjectives, they describe nouns: *the dog which is running, the cat that is sleeping, the child who is playing, the restaurant where we ate*. The noun modified by a relative clause is the head noun.

In Klingon, the verb in the relative clause ends with the Type 9 suffix **-bogh,** which will, for convenience, be translated *which*.

Whether the head noun follows or precedes the relative clause depends on its relationship to that clause. Compare the following:

qIppu'bogh yaS *officer who hit him/her*
yaS qIppu'bogh *officer whom he/she hit*

In both phrases, the relative clause is **qIppu'bogh** (**qIp** *hit,* **-pu'** *perfective,* **-bogh** *which*), and the head noun is **yaS** *officer*. In the first phrase, **yaS** is the subject of the verb **qIp** (the officer is doing the hitting), so it follows **qIppu'bogh,** just as all subjects follow the verb. In the second phrase, **yaS** is the object (the officer is getting hit), so it precedes **qIppu'bogh**, just as all objects precede the verb.

The whole construction (relative clause plus head noun), as a unit, is used in a sentence as a noun. Accordingly, this construction follows or precedes the verb of the sentence, depending on whether it is the subject or object.

> **qIppu'bogh yaS vIlegh** *I see the officer who hit him/her.*

The entire relative construction **qIppu'bogh yaS** *officer who hit him/her* is the object of the verb **vIlegh** *I see him/her,* so it precedes the verb.

> **mulegh qIppu'bogh yaS** *The officer who hit him/her sees me.*

Here, **qIppu'bogh yaS** is the subject of the verb **mulegh** *he/she sees me,* so it follows the verb.

This pattern is also followed when the head noun is the object of the verb in the relative clause, such as **yaS qIppu'bogh** *officer whom he/she hit.*

> **yaS qIppu'bogh vIlegh** *I see the officer whom he/she hit.*
> **mulegh yaS qIppu'bogh** *The officer whom he/she hit sees me.*

In the English translation, the relative pronouns (*that, which,* etc.) may often be omitted: *I see the officer he/she hit, the officer he/she hit sees me.* In Klingon, however, **-bogh** is mandatory.

6.2.4. Purpose clauses

If an action is being done in order to accomplish something, or for the purpose of accomplishing something, the verb describing what is to be accomplished ends with the Type 9 suffix **-meH,** which may be translated *for, for the purpose of, in order to.* The purpose clause always precedes the noun or verb whose purpose it is describing.

> **ja'chuqmeH rojHom neH jaghla'** *The enemy commander wishes a truce (in order) to confer.*

64

The phrase **ja'chuqmeH rojHom** *a truce (in order) to confer* is the object of the verb **neH** *he/she wants it;* the subject is **jaghla'** *enemy commander.* The object is a noun **rojHom** *truce* preceded by the purpose clause **ja'chuqmeH** *for the purpose of conferring* or *in order to confer.* (The verb is made up of **ja'** *tell,* **-chuq** *each other;* thus, *confer* is *tell each other.*)

> **jagh luHoHmeH jagh lunejtaH** *They are searching for the enemy in order to kill him/her.*

Here the purpose clause is **jagh luHoHmeH** *in order for them to kill the enemy,* which is made up of the object noun **jagh** *enemy* preceding the verb **luHoHmeH** *in order for them to kill him/her* (**lu-** *they–him/her,* **HoH** *kill,* **-meH** *for*). It describes the purpose of the verb **lunejtaH** *they are searching for him/her* (**lu-** *they–him/her,* **nej** *seek, search for,* **-taH** *continuous*). Note that, just as in compound sentences, the object noun **jagh** *enemy* occurs before each verb for which it is the object. Thus, somewhat more literally, the sentence may be translated *In order to kill the enemy, they are searching for the enemy.*

Furthermore, just as in compound sentences, the second of two identical nouns may be replaced by a pronoun or, if the context is clear, left out altogether.

> **jagh luHoHmeH ghaH lunejtaH**
> **jagh luHoHmeH lunejtaH** *They are searching for the enemy in order to kill him/her.*

6.2.5. Sentences as objects

Klingon has two special pronouns, **'e'** and **net,** which refer to the previous sentence as a whole. They are used primarily, though not exclusively, with verbs of thinking or observation (such as *know, see*). They are always treated as the object of the verb, and the verb always takes a prefix indicating a third-person singular object. What is a single sentence in English is often two sentences in Klingon. **net** is used only under special circumstances (see page 66), but **'e'** is common. Several examples should make the use of **'e'** clear.

qama'pu' DIHoH 'e' luSov *They know we kill prisoners.*

This sentence is actually two: (1) **qama'pu' DIHoH** *We kill prisoners* (**qama'pu'** *prisoners*, **DIHoH** *we kill them*); (2) **'e' luSov** *They know that* (**'e'** *that*, **luSov** *they know it*). The pronoun **'e'** refers to the previous sentence, *We kill prisoners.*

yaS qIppu' 'e' vIlegh *I saw him/her hit the officers.*

The two sentences here are: (1) **yaS qIppu'** *He/she hit the officer;* (2) **'e' vIlegh** *I see that* (**vIlegh** *I see it*). The construction might equally well be translated as *I saw that he/she hit the officer.* Note that the verb in the second sentence, **vIlegh** *I see it*, is neutral as to time. The past tense of the translation (*I saw . . .*) comes from the verb in the first sentence, **qIppu'** *he/she hit him/her* (**-pu'** *perfective*). In complex sentences of this type, the second verb never takes an aspect suffix (section 4.2.7).

When the verb of the second sentence has a third-person subject (that is, the pronominal prefix is 0) but the intended meaning is *one* or *someone*, rather than *he, she, it,* or *they,* **net** is used instead of **'e'**.

qama'pu' DIHoH net Sov *One knows we kill prisoners.*

As above, the first sentence here is **qama'pu' DIHoH** *We kill prisoners.* The second sentence is **net Sov** *One knows that.* The full construction implies that it is common knowledge that the group to which the speaker belongs kills prisoners.

Qu'vaD lI' net tu'bej *One certainly finds it useful for the mission.*

The first part of this example is **Qu'vaD lI'** *It is useful for the mission* (**Qu'vaD** *for the mission*, **lI'** *it is useful*). The second part is **net tu'bej** *One certainly finds that* or *One certainly observes that.* The full construction might also be translated *One will certainly observe that it is useful to the mission.* Note that although the word *will* makes a more flowing translation, there is nothing in the Klingon sentence indicating future tense.

When the verb of the second sentence is **neH** *want,* neither 'e' nor **net** is used, but the construction is otherwise identical to that just described.

> **jIQong vIneH** *I want to sleep.*
> (**jIQong** *I sleep,* **vIneH** *I want it*)

> **qalegh vIneH** *I want to see you.*
> (**qalegh** *I see you,* **vIneH** *I want it*)

> **Dalegh vIneH** *I want you to see him/her.*
> (**Dalegh** *you see him/her,* **vIneH** *I want it*)

> **qama'pu' vIjonta' vIneH** *I wanted to capture prisoners.*

In this final example, the first part is **qama'pu' vIjonta'** *I captured prisoners* (**qama'pu'** *prisoners,* **vIjonta'** *I captured them*). Note once again that the aspect marker (in this case, **-ta'** *accomplished*) goes with the first verb only; the second verb, **vIneH** *I want it,* is neutral as to time. The past tense of the translation *(I wanted . . .)* comes from the aspect marker on the first verb.

Similarly, with verbs of saying (*say, tell, ask,* etc.), **'e'** and **net** are not used. The two phrases simply follow one another, in either order.

> **qaja'pu' HIqaghQo'**
> or **HIqaghQo' qaja'pu'** *I told you not to interrupt me.*

This is literally *I told you, "Don't interrupt me!"* or *"Don't interrupt me" I told you* (**qaja'pu'** *I told you,* **HIqaghQo'** *don't interrupt me!*). An aspect marker (here, **-pu'** *perfective*) may always be attached to the verb of saying, regardless of whether it is the first or second verb.

Finally, the use of **rIntaH** to indicate that an action is accomplished (section 4.2.7) is another example of the two-verb (or two-sentence) construction.

6.3. "To be"

There is no verb corresponding to English *to be* in Klingon. On the other hand, all pronouns (section 5.1) can be used as verbs, in the sense of *I am, you are,* etc.

> **tlhIngan jIH** *I am a Klingon.*

yaS SoH *You are an officer.*
puqpu' chaH *They are children.*

The pronoun always follows the noun.

Similarly, there is no verb corresponding to *to be* in the sense of "to be at a place." Again, the pronouns are used, followed, where appropriate, by verbal suffixes.

pa'wIjDaq jIHtaH *I am in my quarters.*
(**pa'wIjDaq** *in my room,* **jIH** *I,*
-taH *continuous*)

In the above examples, the subjects are pronouns. If the subject is a noun, it follows the third-person pronoun (**ghaH** *he/she,* **'oH** *it,* **chaH** *they,* **bIH** *they*) and takes the **-'e'** *topic* suffix (see section 3.3.5).

puqpu' chaH qama'pu' 'e' *The prisoners are children.*
pa'DajDaq ghaHtaH la''e' *The commander is in his quarters.*

These sentences might also be translated *As for the prisoners, they are children; As for the commander, he is in his quarters.*

6.4. Questions

There are two types of questions: those which may be answered "yes" or "no," and those which require explanations as answers.

Yes/no questions are formed with the Type 9 suffix **-'a'** added to the verb. Examples are given in section 4.2.9.

Appropriate answers to yes/no questions are:

HIja' or **HISlaH** *yes*
ghobe' *no*

The other type of question contains a question word:

chay' *how?*
ghorgh *when?*
nuq *what?*
nuqDaq *where?*

qatlh *why?*
'ar *how many? how much?*
'Iv *who?*

For **'Iv** *who?* and **nuq** *what?* the question word fits into the sentence in the position that would be occupied by the answer. For example:

> **yaS legh 'Iv** *Who sees the officer?*
> **'Iv legh yaS** *Whom does the officer see?*

In the first question, it is the subject which is being asked about, so **'Iv** *who?* goes in the subject position, following the verb **legh** *he/she sees him/her.* In the second case, the object is being questioned, so the question word goes in the object position, before the verb.

Similarly with **nuq** *what?:*

> **Duj ghoStaH nuq** *What is coming toward the ship?*
> (**Duj** *ship, vessel,* **ghoStaH** *it is*
> *proceeding toward it*)
> **nuq legh yaS** *What does the officer see?*

Both **'Iv** and **nuq** are treated as nouns as far as the pronominal prefixes are concerned. That is, they are considered third person.

> **nughoStaH nuq** *What is coming toward us?* (**nughoStaH** *it*
> *is proceeding toward us*)
> **nuq Dalegh** *What do you see?* (**Dalegh** *you see it*)

The word for *where?*, **nuqDaq**, is actually **nuq** *what?* followed by the suffix **-Daq** *locative* (see section 3.3.5). As would any locative phrase (see section 6.1), it comes at the beginning of the sentence.

> **nuqDaq So'taH yaS** *Where is the officer hiding?*
> (**So'taH** *he/she is hiding*)

Three other question words likewise occur at the beginning of the sentence.

ghorgh Haw'pu' yaS *When did the officer flee?*
          (**Haw'pu'** *he/she has fled*)
qatlh Haw'pu' yaS *Why did the officer flee?*
chay' Haw'pu' yaS *How did the officer flee?*

Note also:

      chay' jura' *What are your orders?*

This is actually **chay'** *how?*, **jura'** *you command us;* thus, *How do you command us?*

The question word **chay'** *how?* may be used as a one-word sentence meaning *How did this happen? What happened? What the—?*

Finally, **'ar** *how many? how much?* follows the noun to which it refers. It can never follow a noun with a plural suffix (**-pu'**, **-mey**, **-Du'**; see section 3.3.2).

    Haw'pu' yaS 'ar *How many officers fled?*
                (**Haw'pu'** *they fled,* **yaS** *officer*)
    nIn 'ar wIghaj *How much fuel do we have?*
              (**nIn** *fuel,* **wIghaj** *we have it*)

6.5. Commands

Commands are given with appropriate imperative prefixes. See sections 4.1.2, 4.3.

6.6. Comparatives and superlatives

The idea of something being more or greater than something else (comparative) is expressed by means of a construction which can be represented by the following formula:

$$A \ Q \ \text{law'} \ B \ Q \ \text{puS}$$

In this formula, A and B are the two things being compared and Q is the quality which is being measured. The two Klingon words in the formula are **law'** *be many* and **puS** *be few.* Thus, it says *A's Q is many, B's Q is few* or *A has more Q than B has* or *A is Q-er than B.*

Any verb expressing a quality or condition may fit into the Q slot.

la' jaq law' yaS jaq puS *The commander is bolder than the officer.*
(**la'** *commander,* **jaq** *be bold,* **yaS** *officer*)

To express the superlative, that something is the most or the greatest of all, the noun **Hoch** *all* is used in the B position:

la' jaq law' Hoch jaq puS *The commander is boldest of all.*

In comparative and superlative constructions, the verb of quality (**jaq** *be bold* in the sentences above) must be said twice.

7. CLIPPED KLINGON

The preceding grammatical sketch describes "proper" Klingon, that is, Klingon as it is taught in Klingon schools or to non-Klingons. In actual day-to-day use, however, spoken Klingon may vary somewhat from its "proper" form, usually by leaving some elements out. This abbreviated form of speaking, called Clipped Klingon by Klingon grammarians, is heard quite frequently in military contexts where quick —rather than eloquent—communication is deemed a virtue. Probably for similar reasons, Clipped Klingon is used quite extensively in all walks of Klingon life.

Some of the features of Clipped Klingon are described below.

7.1. Commands

In giving commands, the imperative prefix (section 4.1.2) may be left off, leaving the bare verb.

Proper Klingon: **yIbaH** *Fire (the torpedoes)!*
Clipped Klingon: **baH**

Proper Klingon: **wIy yIcha'** *Show the tactical display!*
Clipped Klingon: **wIy cha'**
    (**wIy** *tactical display on monitor*, **cha'** *show, project*)

Proper Klingon: **He chu' yIghoS** *Follow a new course!*

Clipped Klingon: **He chu' ghoS**
    (**He** *course,* **chu'** *be new,* **ghoS** *follow a course*)

When the object noun is critical, and what is to be done with that noun is obvious (or should be obvious) to the listener, that noun itself may serve as the command.

Proper Klingon: **chuyDaH yIlaQ** *Fire the thrusters!*
Clipped Klingon: **chuyDaH** *Thrusters!*
    (**chuyDaH** *thrusters,* **laQ** *fire, energize*)

Proper Klingon: **HaSta yIcha'** *Show the visual display!*
Clipped Klingon: **HaSta** *Visual (display)!*
    (**HaSta** *visual display on monitor,* **cha'** *show,
    project*)

Finally, other grammatical markers, particularly noun suffixes, may be left out of commands.

Proper Klingon: **jolpa'Daq yIjaH** *Go to the transport room!*
Clipped Klingon: **jolpa' yIjaH**
    (**jolpa'** *transport room,* **-Daq** *locative,* **jaH** *go*)

It is not common, when noun suffixes are chopped, for the imperative prefix on the verb to be dropped as well.

7.2. Responses to commands, status reports

Responses to commands and status reports are also prone to clipping.

Proper Klingon: **So'wI' vIchu'ta'** *I have engaged the cloak-
                ing device.*
Proper Klingon: **So'wI' chu'lu'ta'** *The cloaking device
                has been engaged.*
Clipped Klingon: **So'wI' chu'ta'** *Cloaking device engaged.*
    (**So'wI'** *cloaking device,* **vIchu'ta'** *I have engaged it,*
    chu'lu'ta' *it has been engaged*)

In the preceding example, the clipped form can correspond to either a dropping of the prefix **vI-** *I–it* or the suffix **-lu'** *indefinite subject.*

Proper Klingon: **jIyajchu'** *I understand clearly.*
Clipped Klingon: **yajchu'** *Understood clearly.*
    (**yaj** *understand,* **-chu'** *clearly, perfectly*)

73

In this final example, the clipped form, lacking the pronominal prefix **jI-** *I,* is a likely response to a question in clipped form, such as **yaj'a'** *Understood?* (compare Proper Klingon **bIyaj'a'** *Do you understand?*).

7.3. Duress, excitement

When in a situation of great danger or when immediate action may be necessary, a Klingon is apt to drop pronominal prefixes. This clipped form is also common when a Klingon is excited for some reason.

Proper Klingon: **qama'pu' vIjonta' vIneH** *I wanted to capture prisoners.*

Clipped Klingon: **qama'pu' jonta' neH** *Wanted prisoners!* (**qama'pu'** *prisoners,* **vIjonta'** *I captured them,* **vIneH** *I want them*)

In context, it would be clear that the speaker is the one doing the wanting (and capturing), even though the pronominal prefix **vI-** *I–them* is missing.

DICTIONARY

INTRODUCTORY REMARKS

The dictionary contains four parts: (1) Klingon to English, (2) English to Klingon, (3) list of affixes in Klingon alphabetical order, (4) list of affixes in English alphabetical order.

Klingon alphabetical order is as follows:

**a, b, ch, D, e, gh, H, I, j, l, m, n, ng,
o, p, q, Q, r, S, t, tlh, u, v, w, y, '**

Note that **ch, gh, ng,** and **tlh** are considered separate letters. Thus the syllable **no** would precede the syllable **nga** in the Klingon list.

Each Klingon word is tagged as to type (noun, verb, etc.). This tag occurs at the end of the English translation. The abbreviations used to indicate word types are:

adv	adverbial	(section 5.4)
conj	conjunction	(section 5.3)
excl	exclamation	(section 5.5)
n	noun	(section 3)
num	number	(section 5.2)
pro	pronoun	(section 5.1)
ques	question word	(section 6.4)
v	verb	(section 4)

In looking through the dictionary, it will be noticed that there are a number of noun/verb pairs; that is, the same word is both a noun and a verb. Futhermore, there are some words which are identical in form (and nearly identical in meaning) to some suffixes (for example, **laH** is a noun meaning *accomplishment* and **-laH** is a verb suffix meaning *can, able*).

There are also a number of Klingon synonyms; that is two Klingon words with identical meanings (for example, **joh, jaw** *lord*, **chetvI', DuS** *torpedo tube*). Occasionally one member of such a synonym set can be analyzed. Thus, **baHwI'** *gunner* consists of the verb **baH** *fire (a torpedo)* plus the suffix **-wI'** *one who does something*. The other word for *gunner*, **matha'**, remains impervious to analysis. Sometimes one member of a set may be partially analyzed. For example, **jonta'** *engine* begins with **jon**, which is also found in **jonwI'** *engineer*, and ends with **ta'**, which also occurs in **mIqta'** *machinery*. The other members of these synonym sets, **QuQ** *engine* and **jo'** *machinery*, cannont be further analyzed. (It is likely that there are sets of synonyms with three or more members, but none has been found to date.)

It has not yet been possible to determine how, or whether, the synonyms are used differentially. Perhaps there is a suggestion of Klingon social structure hidden here, for many of the synonym sets are words relating to military or governmental rank (such as **yaS, 'utlh** *officer*). On the other hand, some of the pairings are words referring to mechanics or engineering (such as *engine* and *torpedo tube,* as illustrated above). Perhaps a more thorough understanding of Klingon technology would reveal that there is indeed a difference in meaning among members of each set. Despite the current incomplete understanding of synonyms, the student of Klingon can be relatively assured that no major social blunder will be committed by choosing one rather than the other member of a synonym set.

These various pairings (noun/verb, word/suffix, synonym sets) are of great historical interest, for they surely indicate something about earlier stages of the language. Unfortunately, a linguistic history of Klingon is beyond the scope of the present work.

For ease of reference, English entries in the English-

INTRODUCTORY REMARKS

Klingon section of this dictionary begin with the word that the user would most likely be looking for, even though this may at times be grammatically incorrect. This first word is, when appropriate, followed by the correct translation. For example, English adjectives (e.g., *bold*) correspond to Klingon verbs, most accurately translated using the English verb *to be* (e.g., *be bold*). All such words are entered with the adjective first, followed by the accurate translation (e.g., *bold, be bold*). Similarly, when a Klingon word is translated into an English phrase (e.g., *have a headache*), the first word in the English entry is the key word in the phrase, followed by the proper translation (e.g., *headache, have a headache*).

KLINGON-ENGLISH

bach	shoot (v)
bach	shot (n)
baH	fire (torpedo, rocket, missile) (v)
baHwI'	gunner (n)
bang	love, one who is loved (n)
baS	metal (n)
batlh	honor (n)
batlh	honored, with honor (adv)
bav	orbit (v)
ba'	sit (v)
bech	suffer (v)
begh	deflectors (n)
beH	rifle (n)
bej	watch (v)
bel	be pleased (v)
bel	pleasure (n)
belHa'	be displeased (v)
ben	years ago (n)
bep	agony (n)
bep	complain, object, gripe (v)
beq	crew, crewman (n)
bergh	be irritable (v)
be'	female, woman (n)

be'Hom	girl (n)
be'nal	wife (n)
be'nI'	sister (n)
bID	half (n)
bIghHa'	prison, jail (n)
bIH	they, them (incapable of language) (pro)
bIng	area below, area under (n)
bIp	hundred thousand (num)
bIQ	water (n)
bIQtIq	river (n)
bIQ'a'	ocean (n)
bIr	be cold (v)
bIt	be nervous, uneasy (v)
bIv	break (rules) (v)
bobcho'	module (n)
boch	shine, be shiny (v)
bogh	be born (v)
boH	be impatient (v)
boj	nag (v)
bong	accidentally, by accident (adv)
boq	alliance (n)
boQ	aide (n)
boQ	assist (v)
boQDu'	aide-de-camp (n)
bortaS	revenge (n)
boS	collect (v)
bot	prevent, block, prohibit (v)
botlh	center, middle (n)
bov	era (n)
bo'DIj	court (n)
buD	be lazy (v)
bup	quit (v)
buQ	threaten (v)
burgh	stomach (n)
buS	concentrate on, focus on, think only about (v)
butlh	dirt under fingernails (n)
buv	classification (n)
buv	classify (v)
bu'	sergeant (n)

cha	torpedoes (n)
chach	emergency (n)
chagh	drop (v)
chaH	they, them (capable of using language) (pro)
chal	sky(n)
chamwI'	technician (n)
chap	back (of hand) (n)
chaq	perhaps (adv)
chargh	conquer (v)
chav	achieve (v)
chav	achievement (n)
chaw'	allow, permit (v)
chay'	how? (ques)
cha'	show, display (picture) (v)
cha'	two (num)
cha'DIch	second (num)
cha'Hu'	day before yesterday (n)
cha'leS	day after tomorrow (n)
cha'logh	twice (adv)
cha'puj	dilithium (n)
cha'pujqut	dilithium crystal (n)
chech	be drunk, intoxicated (v)
chegh	return (v)
cheH	defect (v)
chel	add (v)
chen	build up, take form (v)
chep	prosper, be prosperous (v)
cher	establish, set up (v)
chergh	tolerate (v)
chetvI'	torpedo tube (n)
chev	separate (v)
che'	rule, reign, run (v)
chIch	purposely, on purpose, intentionally (adv)
chID	admit (v)
chIj	navigate (v)
chIjwI'	navigator (n)
chIm	be empty, deserted, uninhabited (v)
chIp	cut, trim (hair) (v)

chIrgh	temple (structure) (n)
chIS	be white (v)
choH	alter, change (v)
choH	change (n)
chol	close in, get closer, come nearer (v)
choljaH	ponytail holder (n)
chom	bartender (n)
chong	be vertical (v)
chop	bite (v)
choq	preserve (v)
chor	belly (n)
chorgh	eight (num)
chorghDIch	eighth (num)
choS	desert (v)
choS	twilight (n)
chot	murder (v)
chovnatlh	specimen (n)
chuch	ice (n)
chun	be innocent (v)
chunDab	meteor (n)
chung	accelerate (v)
chup	recommend, suggest (v)
chuq	range, distance (n)
chuQun	nobility (n)
chuS	be noisy (v)
chut	law (n)
chuv	be left over (v)
chuvmey	leftovers (grammatical term) (n)
chuyDaH	thrusters (n)
chu'	be new (v)
chu'	engage, activate (a device) (v)
Dach	be absent (v)
DaH	now (adv)
Daj	be interesting (v)
Dal	be boring (v)
Dan	occupy (military term) (v)
Dap	nonsense (n)
Daq	eavesdrop (v)
DaQ	ponytail (n)

83

DaS	boot (n)
DaSpu'	boot spike (n)
Dat	everywhere (n)
Daw'	revolt (v)
Daw'	revolt, revolution (n)
Da'	corporal (rank) (n)
Deb	desert (n)
Dech	surround (v)
Degh	helm (n)
DeghwI'	helmsman (n)
Dej	collapse (v)
Del	describe (v)
DenIb	Denebia (n)
DenIbngan	Denebian (n)
DenIb Qatlh	Denebian slime devil (n)
Dep	being (nonhumanoid) (n)
DeQ	credit (monetary unit) (n)
DeS	arm (body part) (n)
Dev	lead, guide (v)
De'	data, information (n)
De'wI'	computer (n)
DIb	privilege (n)
DIch	certainty (n)
DIl	pay for (v)
DIlyum	trillium (n)
DIng	spin (v)
DIp	noun (n)
DIr	skin (n)
DIS	cave (n)
DIS	confess (v)
DIS	year (Klingon) (n)
DIv	be guilty (v)
DIvI'	federation, organization (n)
DIvI'may'Duj	Federation battle cruiser (n)
Do	velocity (n)
Doch	be rude (v)
Doch	thing (n)
Dogh	be foolish, silly (v)
Doghjey	unconditional surrender (n)
DoH	back away from, back off, get away from (v)

Doj	be impressive (v)
Dol	entity (n)
Dom	radan (crude dilithium crystal) (n)
Don	be parallel, go parallel to (v)
Dop	side (n)
Doq	be orange, red (v)
DoQ	claim (territory) (v)
Dor	escort (v)
DoS	target (n)
Dotlh	status (n)
Doy'	be tired (v)
Doy'yuS	Troyius (n)
Do'	be fortunate, lucky (v)
Do'	luckily, with luck (adv)
Dub	back (of body) (n)
Dub	improve (v)
DuD	mix (v)
Dugh	be vigilant (v)
DuH	be possible (v)
DuH	possibility, option (n)
Duj	instincts (n)
Duj	ship, vessel (n)
Dum	nap (v)
Dun	be wonderful, great (v)
Dung	area above, area overhead (n)
Dup	strategy (n)
DuQ	stab (v)
DuS	torpedo tube (n)
DuSaQ	school (n)
Duv	advance (v)
Duy	agent, emissary (n)
Duy'	be defective (v)
Duy'	defect (n)
Du'	farm (n)
ghagh	gargle (v)
ghaH	he, she, him, her (pro)
ghaj	have, possess (v)
ghap	or, either/or (joining nouns) (conj)
ghaq	contribute (v)

ghar	conduct diplomacy (v)
ghar	diplomacy (n)
ghargh	serpent, worm (n)
gharwI'	diplomat (n)
ghatlh	dominate (v)
ghegh	be rough (v)
ghem	midnight snack (n)
ghIb	consent (v)
ghIch	nose (n)
ghIgh	necklace (n)
ghIH	be messy, sloppy (v)
ghIj	scare (v)
ghIm	exile (v)
ghIpDIj	court-martial (v)
ghIQ	vacation, take a vacation (v)
ghIr	descend (v)
ghItlh	manuscript (n)
ghItlh	write (v)
gho	circle (n)
ghob	ethics (n)
ghobe'	no (answer to a question) (excl)
ghoch	destination (n)
ghoD	stuff (v)
ghogh	voice (n)
ghoH	argue, dispute (v)
ghoj	learn (v)
ghojmoH	teach, instruct (v)
ghojwI'	student (n)
ghol	opponent, adversary (n)
ghom	group, party (n)
ghom	meet, encounter, assemble, rendez-vous (v)
ghomHa'	scatter, disperse (v)
ghom'a'	crowd (n)
ghong	abuse (n)
ghong	abuse (v)
ghop	hand (n)
ghopDap	asteroid (n)
ghoq	spy (v)
ghoqwI'	spy (n)
ghor	break (v)

ghor	surface (of a planet) (n)
ghorgh	when? (ques)
ghoS	approach, go away from, proceed, come, follow (a course) (v)
ghoS	thrust (v)
ghot	person (humanoid) (n)
ghov	recognize (v)
gho'	step on (v)
gho'Do	sublight speed (n)
ghu	baby (n)
ghuH	alert (n)
ghuH	prepare for, be alerted to (v)
ghuHmoH	alert, warn (v)
ghum	alarm (n)
ghum	alarm, sound an alarm (v)
ghun	program (a computer) (v)
ghung	be hungry (v)
ghup	swallow (v)
ghur	increase (v)
ghuS	be prepared, ready (to launch) (v)
ghu'	situation (n)
Hab	be smooth (v)
HablI'	data transceiving device (n)
Hach	be developed (e.g., civilization) (v)
HaD	study (v)
Hagh	laugh (v)
Haj	dread (v)
Hal	source (n)
HanDogh	nacelle (n)
Hap	matter (n)
Haq	surgery (n)
HaQchor	saccharin (n)
Har	believe (v)
HaSta	visual display (n)
Hat	be illegal (v)
Hat	temperature (n)
Hatlh	country, countryside (n)
Haw'	flee, get out (v)
Hay'	duel (v)
Ha'	let's go, come on (excl)

Ha'DIbaH	animal (n)
He	course, route (n)
Hech	intend, mean to (v)
HeD	retreat (v)
HeDon	parallel course (n)
Hegh	die (v)
HeghmoH	be fatal (v)
HeH	edge (n)
Hej	rob (v)
Hem	be proud (v)
HeQ	comply (v)
Hergh	medicine (n)
HeS	commit a crime (v)
HeS	crime (n)
HeSwI'	criminal (n)
Hev	receive (v)
He'	smell, emit odor (v)
He'So'	stink (v)
HIch	handgun (n)
HIchDal	airlock (n)
HIDjolev	menu (n)
HIgh	fight dirty (v)
HIja'	yes, true (answer to yes/no question) (excl)
HIp	uniform (n)
HIq	liquor (n)
HISlaH	yes, true (answer to yes/no question) (excl)
HIv	attack (v)
HIvje'	glass (tumbler) (n)
HI'	dictator (n)
HI'tuy	dictatorship (n)
Hob	yawn (v)
Hoch	everyone, all, everything (n)
HoD	captain (n)
Hogh	week (Klingon) (n)
HoH	kill (v)
HoH'egh	commit suicide (v)
Hoj	be cautious (v)
Hol	language (n)
Hom	bone (n)

Hon	doubt (v)
Hong	impulse power (n)
Hop	be remote, far (v)
Hoq	expedition (n)
Hoqra'	tricorder (n)
HoS	be strong (v)
HoS	strength, energy, power (n)
HoSchem	energy field (n)
HoSDo'	energy beings (n)
HoSghaj	be powerful (v)
Hot	touch, feel (v)
Hotlh	project, put on (screen) (v)
Hotlh	scan (v)
HotlhwI'	scanner (n)
Hov	star (n)
Hovtay'	star system (n)
Hoy'	congratulate (v)
Ho'	admire (v)
Ho'	tooth (n)
Ho"oy'	toothache (n)
Hu	zoo (n)
Hub	defend (v)
Hub	defense (n)
Huch	money (n)
HuD	mountain, hill (n)
Hugh	throat (n)
Huj	be strange (v)
Huj	charge (up) (v)
Hum	be sticky (v)
Human	human (n)
Hung	security (n)
Hup	punish (v)
Huq	transact (v)
Hur	outside (n)
Hurgh	be dark (v)
Hurgh	pickle (cucumber) (n)
HuS	hang (v)
Hut	nine (num)
HutDIch	ninth (num)
Huv	be clear, not obstructed (v)
Huy'	eyebrow (n)

Hu'	days ago (n)
Hu'	get up (v)
jab	serve (food) (v)
jabbI'ID	data transmission (n)
jach	scream, cry out, shout, yell (v)
jagh	enemy (n)
jaH	go (v)
jaj	day (from dawn to dawn) (n)
jajlo'	dawn (n)
jan	device (n)
jang	answer, reply (v)
jaq	be bold (v)
jar	month (Klingon) (n)
jat	tongue (n)
jatlh	speak (v)
jav	six (num)
javDIch	sixth (num)
jaw	chat (v)
jaw	lord (n)
ja'	tell, report (v)
ja'chuq	discuss, confer (v)
je	also, and (joining nouns) (conj)
jech	disguise (v)
jegh	surrender, give up (v)
jeH	be absentminded (v)
jej	be sharp (v)
jen	be high (v)
jeQ	be self-confident (v)
jeS	participate (v)
jev	storm (v)
jey	defeat (v)
je'	buy, purchase (v)
je'	feed (someone else) (v)
jIb	hair (on head) (n)
jIH	I, me (pro)
jIH	viewing screen (n)
jIj	cooperate (v)
jIl	neighbor (n)
jInmol	project (n)
jIp	penalty (n)

jIv	be ignorant (v)
jo	resources (n)
joch	be harmful (v)
joD	stoop (v)
joH	lord (n)
joj	area between (n)
jojlu'	consul (n)
jol	beam (aboard) (v)
jol	transport beam (n)
jolpa'	transport room (n)
jolvoy'	transporter ionizer unit (n)
jon	capture (v)
jonta'	engine (n)
jonwI'	engineer (n)
joq	flap, flutter, wave (v)
joq	or, and/or (joining nouns) (conj)
joqwI'	flag (n)
jor	explode (v)
jorwI'	explosive (n)
joS	gossip (v)
joS	rumor, gossip (n)
jot	be calm (v)
jotHa'	be uneasy (v)
jotlh	take down (v)
joy'	torture (v)
jo'	machinery (n)
jub	be immortal (v)
jubbe'	be mortal (v)
juH	home (n)
jum	be odd (v)
jun	evade, take evasive action (v)
jup	friend (n)
juS	overtake, pass (v)
juv	measure (v)
lab	transmit data (away from a place) (v)
lach	exaggerate (v)
laD	read (v)
laH	ability (n)
laj	accept (v)
laj	acceptance (n)

91

lalDan	religion (n)
lam	be dirty (v)
lam	dirt (n)
lan	place (v)
lang	be thin (v)
laQ	fire, energize (e.g., thrusters) (v)
largh	smell, sense odors (v)
laSvargh	factory (n)
law'	be many (v)
lay'	promise (v)
la'	commander (n)
legh	see (v)
leH	maintain (v)
leH	maintenance (n)
lel	get out, take out (v)
leng	roam, travel, rove (v)
leng	trip, voyage (n)
lengwI'	rover (grammatical term) (n)
leQ	switch (n)
leS	days from now (n)
leS	rest, relax (v)
leSpoH	shore leave (n)
let	be hard (like a rock) (v)
le'	be special, exceptional (v)
lIgh	ride (v)
lIH	introduce (v)
lIj	forget (v)
lIm	panic (v)
lInDab	espionage (n)
lIng	produce (v)
lIq	round up (v)
lIS	adjust (v)
lIy	comet (n)
lI'	be useful (v)
lI'	transmit data (to a place) (v)
lob	obey (v)
lobHa'	disobey (v)
loch	mustache (n)
loD	male, man (n)
loDHom	boy (n)
loDnal	husband (n)

loDnI'	brother (n)
logh	space (n)
loH	administer (v)
loH	administration (n)
loj	be all gone (v)
lojmIt	door, gate (n)
lolSeHcha	attitude-control thrusters (n)
lom	corpse (n)
lon	abandon (v)
lop	celebrate (v)
loQ	slightly, a little bit (adv)
loS	four (num)
loS	wait (for) (v)
loSDIch	fourth (num)
loSpev	quadrotriticale (n)
lot	catastrophe (n)
lotlh	rebel (v)
lotlhwI'	rebel (n)
loy	guess (v)
lo'	use (v)
lo'laH	be valuable (v)
lo'laHbe'	be worthless (v)
luch	equipment, gear (n)
lugh	be right, correct (v)
luH	yank (v)
luj	fail (v)
lulIgh	refuge (n)
lum	postpone, procrastinate (v)
lup	second (of time) (n)
lup	transport (v)
luq	yes, okay, I will (excl)
lur	pupil (of eye) (n)
lurDech	tradition (n)
lut	story (n)
lutlh	be primitive (v)
lu'	yes, okay, I will (excl)
mab	treaty (n)
mach	be small (v)
magh	betray (v)
maghwI'	traitor (n)

maH	ten (number-forming element) (num)
maH	we, us (pro)
maj	good (expressing satisfaction) (excl)
majQa'	well done, very good (excl)
malja'	business (n)
mang	soldier (n)
mangghom	army (n)
maq	proclaim (v)
maS	moon (n)
maS	prefer (v)
maSwov	moonlight (n)
matHa'	gunner (n)
mavjop	paper clip (n)
maw	offend (v)
maw'	be crazy (v)
may	be fair (v)
may'	battle (n)
may'Duj	battle cruiser (n)
may'morgh	battle array (n)
ma'	accommodate (v)
meb	guest (n)
mech	trade (v)
megh	lunch (n)
meH	bridge (of a ship) (n)
mem	catalog (n)
mep	plastic (n)
meq	reason (n)
meq	reason (v)
meQ	burn (v)
mer	surprise (v)
mev	stop, cease (v)
mIch	sector, zone (n)
mID	colony (n)
mIgh	be evil (v)
mIm	delay (v)
mIn	eye (n)
mIp	be rich (v)
mIqta'	machinery (n)
mIr	chain (n)
mIS	be confused, mixed up (v)
mIS	confusion (n)

mISmoH	confuse (v)
mIv	helmet (n)
mIy	brag (v)
mI'	number (n)
mob	be alone (v)
moch	superior (n)
moD	hurry (v)
mogh	be frustrated (v)
moH	be ugly (v)
moHaq	prefix (n)
moj	become (v)
mojaq	suffix (n)
mol	bury (v)
mol	grave (n)
mon	capital (of a place) (n)
mong	neck (n)
mongDech	collar (n)
mop	robe (n)
moQ	sphere (n)
moS	compromise (v)
motlh	be usual (v)
motlhbe'	be unusual (v)
moy'bI'	slingshot (n)
mo'	cage (n)
mub	be legal (v)
much	present (v)
much	presentation (n)
muD	atmosphere (n)
mugh	translate (v)
mughato'	mugato (n)
mughwI'	translator (n)
muH	execute, put to death (v)
muj	be wrong (v)
mul	be stubborn (v)
mung	origin (n)
mup	impact, strike (v)
muS	hate, detest (v)
mut	be selfish (v)
mut	species (n)
muv	join (v)
mu'	word (n)

mu'ghom	dictionary (n)
mu'tay'	vocabulary (n)
mu'tlhegh	sentence (n)
nab	plan (v)
nach	head (n)
naDev	here, hereabouts (n)
nagh	rock, stone (n)
naj	dream (v)
nap	be simple (v)
nargh	appear (v)
naS	be vicious (v)
nav	paper (n)
nawlogh	squadron (n)
naw'	access (v)
nay	marry (wife does this) (v)
nay'	course, dish (at a meal) (n)
nech	be lateral, move laterally (v)
negh	soldiers (n)
neH	only, merely, just (adv)
neH	want (v)
neHmaH	neutral zone (n)
nej	look for, seek, search for (v)
nem	years from now (n)
nep	lie, fib (v)
net	that (previous topic) (pro)
netlh	ten thousand (num)
ne'	yeoman (n)
nIb	be identical (v)
nIch	ammunition (n)
nID	attempt, try (v)
nIH	right (side) (n)
nIH	steal (v)
nIHwI'	thief (n)
nIj	leak (v)
nIn	fuel (n)
nIQ	breakfast (n)
nIS	hinder, interfere (v)
nItlh	finger (n)
nIv	be superior (v)

96

nIvnav	pajamas (n)
nI'	be long, lengthy (duration) (v)
nob	gift (n)
nob	give (v)
noch	sensor (n)
noD	retaliate (v)
nogh	writhe (v)
noH	judge, estimate (v)
noj	lend (v)
nol	funeral (n)
nom	fast, quickly (adv)
non	be rotten (v)
nong	be passionate (v)
nop	omit (v)
noSvagh	deodorant (n)
not	never (adv)
nov	alien, foreigner (n)
nov	be foreign, alien (v)
noy	be famous, well known (v)
no'	ancestors (n)
nub	be suspect (v)
nubwI'	predecessor (n)
nuch	coward (n)
nuD	examine (v)
nugh	society (n)
nuH	weapon (n)
nuHHom	small arms (n)
nuj	mouth (n)
num	promote (v)
nung	precede (v)
nup	decrease (v)
nural	Neural (n)
nuralngan	Neuralese (n)
nuq	what? (ques)
nuqDaq	where? (ques)
nuqneH	what do you want? (greeting) (excl)
nuQ	annoy, bother (v)
nur	dignity (n)
nuS	ridicule (v)
nuv	person (humanoid) (n)

ngab	disappear, vanish (v)
ngach	debate (v)
ngan	inhabitant (n)
ngaq	support (military term) (n)
ngaS	contain (have inside) (v)
ngat	gunpowder (n)
ngav	writer's cramp (n)
ngeb	be counterfeit, false, fake (v)
ngech	valley (n)
ngeD	be easy (v)
ngeH	send (v)
ngej	infect (v)
ngem	forest, woods (n)
ngeng	lake (n)
ngep	override (v)
nger	theory (n)
ngev	sell (v)
nge'	take away (v)
ngIl	dare (v)
ngIm	be putrid (v)
ngIp	borrow (v)
ngIv	patrol (v)
ngoD	fact (n)
ngoH	smear (v)
ngoj	be restless (v)
ngong	experiment (n)
ngong	experiment (v)
ngoq	code (n)
ngoQ	goal (n)
ngor	cheat (v)
ngoS	dissolve (v)
ngotlh	be fanatical (v)
ngoy'	be responsible (v)
ngo'	be old (not new) (v)
ngup	cape (clothing) (n)
ngu'	identify (v)
pab	follow (rules) (v)
pab	grammar (n)
pagh	nothing, none (n)

pagh	or, either/or (joining sentences) (conj)
pagh	zero (num)
paH	gown (n)
paj	resign (v)
paq	book (n)
paQDI'norgh	teachings (n)
par	dislike (v)
parHa'	like (v)
paSlogh	socks (n)
pat	system (n)
pav	be urgent (v)
paw	arrive (v)
paw'	collide (v)
pay	regret (v)
pay'	suddenly (adv)
pa'	room (n)
pa'	there, over there, thereabouts (n)
peD	snow (v)
pegh	keep something secret (v)
pegh	secret (n)
pej	demolish (v)
pem	daytime (n)
pemjep	midday (n)
peng	torpedo (n)
pep	raise (v)
per	label (n)
per	label (v)
pey	acid (n)
pe'	cut (v)
pIch	blame (v)
pIch	fault, blame (n)
pIgh	ruins (n)
pIH	expect (v)
pIH	be suspicious (v)
pIj	often (adv)
pIm	be different (v)
pIn	boss (n)
pIp	spine (n)
pIqaD	Klingon writing system (n)
pItlh	done (excl)

pIv	be healthy (v)
pIvghor	warp drive (n)
pIvlob	warp factor (n)
pI'	be fat (v)
po	morning (n)
pob	hair (on body) (n)
poch	plant (v)
poD	be clipped (v)
pogh	glove (n)
poH	period of time (n)
poH	time (v)
poj	analysis (n)
poj	analyze (v)
pol	keep, save (v)
pom	dysentery (n)
pon	persuade, convince (v)
pong	name (n)
pong	name, call (v)
poq	indigestion (n)
poQ	demand, require (v)
porgh	body (n)
poS	be open, opened (v)
poS	left (side) (n)
poSmoH	open (v)
potlh	consequential thing, something important (n)
pov	afternoon (n)
pov	be excellent (v)
po'	be expert, skilled (v)
pub	boil (v)
puch	toilet (n)
puchpa'	washroom (n)
pugh	dregs (n)
puH	land (n)
puj	be weak (v)
pujmoH	weaken (v)
pujwI'	weakling (n)
pum	accusation (n)
pum	accuse (v)
pum	fall (v)
pung	mercy (n)

pup	be perfect, exact (v)
pup	kick (v)
puq	child, offspring (n)
puqbe'	daughter (n)
puqloD	son (n)
puQ	be fed up (v)
puS	be few, be several, be a handful (v)
puS	sight (with gunsight) (v)
puv	fly (v)
puy	wreck (v)
puyjaq	nova (n)
pu'	phaser (n)
pu'beH	phaser rifle (n)
pu'beq	phaser crew (n)
pu'DaH	phaser banks (n)
pu'HIch	phaser pistol (n)
qab	be bad (v)
qab	face (n)
qach	building, structure (n)
qagh	interrupt (v)
qaH	sir (n)
qal	be corrupt (v)
qalmoH	corrupt (v)
qam	foot (n)
qama'	prisoner (n)
qan	be old (not young) (v)
qap	insist (v)
qaS	occur, happen (v)
qat	wrap (v)
qatlh	why? (ques)
qaw	remember (v)
qawHaq	memory banks (n)
qawmoH	remind (v)
qay'	be a problem, be a hassle (v)
qa'vam	Genesis (n)
qech	idea (n)
qeD	vacate (v)
qeH	resent (v)
qej	be grouchy, mean (v)
qell'qam	kellicam (n)

qem	bring (v)
qempa'	ancestor (n)
qeng	carry, convey (v)
qep	meeting (n)
qeq	drill (military) (n)
qeq	practice, train, prepare (v)
qeS	advice (n)
qeS	advise (v)
qet	run, jog (v)
qetlh	be dull, uninteresting (v)
qev	crowd (v)
qevaS	kevas (n)
qevpob	cheek (n)
qIb	galaxy (n)
qIbHes	galactic rim (n)
qIch	condemn (v)
qIgh	shortcut (n)
qIH	meet (for the first time) (v)
qIj	be black (v)
qIl	cancel (v)
qIm	pay attention, concentrate (v)
qImHa'	disregard (v)
qIp	hit (with hand, fist, implement) (v)
qIQ	mutiny (v)
qIv	knee (n)
qI'	sign (a treaty) (v)
qoch	partner (n)
qogh	belt (n)
qoH	fool (n)
qoj	cliff (n)
qoj	or, and/or (joining sentences) (conj)
qon	record (v)
qop	arrest (v)
qoq	robot (n)
qor	scavenge (v)
qorDu'	family (n)
qotlh	tickle (v)
qoS	birthday (n)
qoy'	plead, beg (v)
qub	be rare (v)
quch	kidnap (v)

qugh	cruise (v)
quHvaj	dandruff (n)
qul	fire (n)
qum	govern (v)
qum	government (n)
qun	history (n)
qun	scold (v)
qup	elder (n)
quprIp	Council of Elders (n)
quq	happen simultaneously (v)
qur	be greedy (v)
quS	chair (n)
qut	crystal (geologic formation) (n)
qu'	be fierce (v)
Qab	theragen (n)
QaD	be dry (v)
Qagh	error, mistake (n)
Qagh	err, be mistaken, make a mistake (v)
QaH	help, aid (v)
Qam	stand (v)
Qan	protect (v)
Qap	work, function, succeed (v)
Qapla'	success (n)
QaQ	be good (v)
Qargh	fissure (n)
QaS	troops (n)
Qat	be popular (v)
Qatlh	be difficult (v)
Qav	be final, last (v)
Qaw'	destroy (n)
Qay	transfer (v)
Qay'	blow one's top (v)
Qa'	type of animal (n)
Qeb	ring (for finger) (n)
QeD	science (n)
QeDpIn	science officer (n)
QeH	anger (n)
QeH	be angry, mad (v)
Qel	doctor, physician (n)
Qey	be tight (v)
QeyHa'	be loose (v)

QeyHa'moH	loosen (v)
QeymoH	tighten (v)
Qe'	restaurant (n)
QIghpej	Klingon agonizer (n)
QIb	shadow (n)
QIch	speech (vocal sounds) (n)
QID	wound (v)
QIH	damage, cause damage (v)
QIH	damage, destruction (n)
QIj	explain (v)
QIp	be stupid (v)
QIt	slowly (adv)
QIv	be inferior (v)
QI'	military (n)
Qob	be dangerous (v)
Qob	danger (n)
Qoch	disagree (v)
Qochbe'	agree (v)
QoD	maneuver (engines) (v)
Qogh	type of animal (n)
Qoj	make war (v)
Qom	experience an earthquake or tremor (v)
QonoS	journal, log (n)
Qong	sleep (v)
Qop	be worn out (v)
QopmoH	wear out (v)
Qorgh	take care of, care for (v)
QoS	be sorry (v)
Qot	lie, recline (v)
Qotlh	disable (v)
Qoy	hear (v)
Qo'	no, I won't, I refuse (excl)
Qub	think (v)
Quch	be happy (v)
Quch	forehead (n)
QuchHa'	be unhappy (v)
QuD	insurrection (n)
Qugh	disaster (n)
Quj	game (n)
Quj	play a game (v)
Qul	research (v)

Qum	communicate (v)
QumpIn	communications officer (n)
QumwI'	communicator, communications device (n)
Qup	be young (v)
QuQ	engine (n)
QuS	conspiracy (n)
QuS	conspire (v)
Qut	be vulgar (v)
Quv	coordinates (n)
Qu'	duty, quest, mission, task, chore (n)
raD	force, compel (v)
ragh	decay (v)
ral	be violent (v)
ram	be trivial, trifling, unimportant (v)
ram	night (n)
ramjep	midnight (n)
rap	be the same (v)
rar	connect (v)
raQ	camp (military term) (n)
raQpo'	passenger (n)
ratlh	remain (v)
rav	floor (n)
ray'	targets (n)
ra'	order, command (v)
ra'wI'	commander (n)
reghuluS	Regulus (n)
reghuluSngan	Regulan (n)
reghuluS 'Iwghargh	Regulan bloodworm (n)
reH	always (adv)
reH	play (v)
rejmorgh	worrywart (n)
rep	hour (n)
retlh	area beside, area next to (n)
rewbe'	citizen (n)
rIgh	be lame (v)
rIH	energize (v)
rIHwI'	energizer (n)
rIn	be accomplished, finished (v)

105

rIp	council, assembly (n)
rIQ	be injured (v)
rIQmoH	injure (v)
rIvSo'	embassy (n)
rIymuS	Remus (n)
ro	trunk (of body) (n)
roghvaH	population (n)
roj	make peace (v)
roj	peace (n)
rojHom	truce (n)
rojmab	peace treaty (n)
rol	beard (n)
rom	accord (n)
romuluS	Romulus (n)
romuluSngan	Romulan (n)
rop	be sick, ill (v)
rop	disease (n)
ropyaH	infirmary (n)
roQ	put down (v)
ror	be fat (v)
rotlh	be tough (v)
ro'	fist (n)
rugh	antimatter (n)
ruQ	control manually, by hand (v)
rup	fine, tax (v)
rur	resemble (v)
rut	sometimes (adv)
ruv	justice (n)
ru'	be temporary (v)
Sab	decline, deteriorate (v)
Sach	expand (v)
SaD	thousand (num)
Sagh	be serious (v)
SaH	be present (not absent) (v)
SaH	care (about), be concerned (about) (v)
Saj	pet (n)
Sal	ascend (v)
San	fate (n)
SanID	thousand (num)
Sang	obliterate (v)

Sap	volunteer (v)
Saq	land (v)
Saqghom	landing party (n)
SaQ	cry (v)
Sar	be varied, various (v)
Sar	variety (n)
Satlh	agriculture (n)
SaS	be horizontal (v)
Saw	marry (husband does this) (v)
Say'	be clean (v)
Sa'	general (rank) (n)
Segh	race (type, sort, class) (n)
SeH	control (v)
SeHlaw	control panel (n)
Seng	cause trouble (v)
Seng	trouble (n)
Sep	breed (v)
Sep	region (n)
Seq	fault (seismic) (n)
Ser	progress (n)
SermanyuQ	Sherman's Planet (n)
SeS	steam (n)
Sev	bandage (n)
Sev	contain (an enemy) (v)
Sey	be excited (v)
SeymoH	excite (v)
Se'	frequency (radio) (n)
SIbDoH	satellite (n)
SIch	reach (v)
SID	patient (n)
SIgh	influence (v)
SIH	bend (v)
SIj	slit (v)
SIm	calculate (v)
SIp	gas (n)
SIQ	endure, bear (v)
SIS	rain (v)
SIv	wonder (v)
Soch	seven (num)
SochDIch	seventh (num)
SoD	flood (n)

107

SoD	flood (v)
SoH	you (pro)
Sol	quarrel (v)
Som	hull (n)
Somraw	muscle (n)
Son	relieve (v)
Sop	eat (v)
SoQ	be closed, shut (v)
SoQ	speech, lecture, address (n)
SoQmoH	close, shut (v)
Sor	tree (n)
Sorgh	sabotage (v)
SoS	mother (n)
SoSnI'	grandmother (n)
Sot	be distressed, be in distress (v)
Sotlaw'	distress call (n)
Sov	know (v)
Soy'	be clumsy (v)
So'	hide, cloak (v)
So'wI'	cloaking device (n)
Sub	be solid (v)
Such	visit (v)
SuD	be green, blue, yellow (v)
SuH	ready, standing by (excl)
Suj	disturb (v)
Sun	discipline (n)
Sung	native (n)
Sup	jump (v)
Sup	resource (n)
Suq	acquire, obtain, get (v)
SuQ	be toxic (v)
Surchem	force field (n)
Surgh	skin (v)
SuS	wind, breeze (n)
Sut	clothing (n)
Sutlh	negotiate (v)
Suv	fight (v)
Suy	merchant (n)
SuyDuj	merchant ship (n)
Su'	ready, standing by (excl)

ta	record (n)
tach	bar, saloon, cocktail lounge (n)
taD	be frozen (v)
taDmoH	freeze (v)
taH	be at a negative angle (v)
taj	knife, dagger (n)
tam	be quiet (v)
tam	exchange, substitute (v)
tammoH	silence (v)
taQ	be weird (v)
taQbang	exhaust (n)
tar	poison (n)
taS	solution (liquid) (n)
tat	ion (n)
tay	be civilized (v)
taymoH	civilize (v)
tayqeq	civilization (n)
tay'	be together (v)
ta'	accomplish (v)
ta'	accomplishment (n)
ta'	emperor (n)
teb	fill (v)
teblaw'	jurisdiction (n)
teH	be true (v)
tej	scientist (n)
tel	wing (n)
telun Hovtay'	Tellun Star System (n)
tem	deny (v)
ten	embark (v)
tengchaH	space station (n)
tep	cargo (n)
tepqengwI'	cargo carrier (n)
teq	remove, take off (v)
tera'	Earth (n)
tera'ngan	Terran, Earther (n)
tet	melt (v)
tev	prize (n)
tey'	confide (v)
tI	vegetation (n)
tIch	insult (v)

tIgh	custom (n)
tIH	ray (n)
tIj	board, go aboard (v)
tIn	be big (v)
tIq	be long, lengthy (of an object) (v)
tIq	heart (n)
tIQ	be ancient (v)
tIr	grain (n)
tIS	be light (weight) (v)
tIv	enjoy (v)
tI'	fix, repair (v)
tob	prove (v)
toch	palm (of hand) (n)
toD	save, rescue (v)
togh	count (v)
toH	so, well (excl)
toj	deceive, trick (v)
tongDuj	freighter (n)
toplIn	topaline (n)
toq	be inhabited (v)
tor	kneel (v)
toS	climb (v)
toy'	serve (a master) (v)
toy'wI'	servant (n)
to'	tactics (n)
tuch	forbid (v)
tugh	soon (adv)
tuH	be ashamed (v)
tuH	maneuver (military term) (n)
tuHmoH	shame (v)
tuj	be hot (v)
tuj	heat (n)
tul	hope (v)
tum	agency (n)
tun	be soft (v)
tung	discourage (v)
tungHa'	encourage (v)
tup	minute (of time) (n)
tuQ	wear (clothes) (v)
tuQDoq	mind sifter (Klingon psychic probe) (n)
tuQHa'moH	undress (v)

tuQmoH	put on (clothes) (v)
tut	column (n)
tuv	be patient (v)
tu'	discover, find, observe, notice (v)
tlhab	be free, independent (v)
tlhab	freedom, independence (n)
tlhap	take (v)
tlhaq	chronometer (n)
tlhaQ	be funny (v)
tlha'	chase, follow (v)
tlheD	depart (v)
tlhegh	line, rope (n)
tlhej	accompany (v)
tlhetlh	progress (v)
tlhe'	turn (v)
tlhIb	be incompetent (v)
tlhIch	smoke (n)
tlhIH	you (plural) (pro)
tlhIl	mine (v)
tlhIl	mineral (n)
tlhIlwI'	miner (n)
tlhIngan	Klingon (n)
tlhIngan wo'	Klingon Empire (n)
tlhIv	be insubordinate (v)
tlhob	ask (v)
tlhoch	contradict (v)
tlhogh	marriage (n)
tlhoj	realize (v)
tlhol	be raw, unprocessed (v)
tlhon	nostril (n)
tlhong	barter, bargain (v)
tlhoQ	conglomeration (n)
tlhov	wheeze (v)
tlhuch	exhaust (v)
tlhuH	breath (n)
tlhuH	breathe (v)
tlhup	whisper (v)
tlhutlh	drink (v)
tlhu'	be tempted (v)
tlhu'moH	tempt (v)

vagh	five (num)
vaghDIch	fifth (num)
vaH	holster (n)
vaj	so, then, thus, in that case (adv)
val	be clever, smart, intelligent (v)
van	salute (v)
vang	act, take action (v)
vaQ	be aggressive (v)
vatlh	hundred (num)
vatlhvI'	percent (n)
vav	father (n)
vavnI'	grandfather (n)
vay'	somebody, something, anybody, anything (n)
veH	boundary (n)
vem	wake up, cease sleeping (v)
vemmoH	wake (someone) up (v)
veng	city (n)
vengHom	village (n)
veQ	garbage (n)
veQDuj	garbage scow (n)
vergh	dock (n)
vergh	dock (v)
veS	war (n)
vetlh	cockroach (n)
vIj	thruster (n)
vIng	whine (v)
vIt	tell the truth (v)
vI'	accumulate (v)
voDleH	emperor (n)
vogh	somewhere (n)
voHDajbo'	ransom (n)
volchaH	shoulder (n)
vong	hypnotize (v)
voq	trust, have faith in (v)
voqHa'	distrust (v)
voQ	choke (v)
vor	cure (v)
vo'	propel (v)
vub	hostage (n)
vuD	opinion (n)

vul	be unconscious (v)
vulqan	Vulcan (planet) (n)
vulqangan	Vulcan (person) (n)
vum	work, toil (v)
vup	pity (v)
vuQ	fascinate (v)
vuS	limit (v)
vut	cook (v)
vutpa'	galley (n)
vuv	respect (v)
vu'	manage (v)
vu'wI'	manager (n)
wam	hunt (v)
wanI'	phenomenon, event, occurrence (n)
waq	shoe (n)
waQ	obstruct (v)
watlh	be pure (v)
wav	divide (v)
waw'	base (military term) (n)
wa'	one (num)
wa'DIch	first (num)
wa'Hu'	yesterday (n)
wa'leS	tomorrow (n)
wa'logh	once (adv)
wa'maH	ten (num)
wa'maHDIch	tenth (num)
web	be disgraced (v)
wegh	confine (v)
weH	raid (v)
wej	not yet (adv)
wej	three (num)
wejDIch	third (num)
wejpuH	charming (used only ironically) (excl)
wem	violate (v)
wem	violation (n)
wep	jacket, coat (n)
wew	glow (v)
wIb	be sour (v)
wIch	myth (n)
wIgh	genius (n)

113

wIH	be ruthless (v)
wIj	farm (v)
wIv	choice (n)
wIv	choose, select (v)
wIy	tactical display (n)
woD	throw away (v)
woH	pick up (v)
woQ	authority, political power (n)
woS	chin (n)
wot	verb (n)
wov	be light, bright (v)
wo'	empire (n)
wuq	decide (v)
wuQ	have a headache (v)
wuS	lip (n)
wutlh	underground (n)
wuv	depend on, rely on (v)
ya	tactical officer (n)
yab	mind, brain (n)
yach	pet, stroke (v)
yaD	toe (n)
yaH	duty station, station (n)
yaj	understand (v)
yajHa'	misinterpret (v)
yap	be enough, sufficient (v)
yaS	officer (n)
yav	ground (n)
yay	victory, triumph (n)
yay'	be shocked, dumbfounded (v)
yej	assembly, council (n)
yem	sin (v)
yep	be careful (v)
yepHa'	be careless (v)
yev	pause (v)
yIb	vent (n)
yIH	tribble (n)
yIn	life (n)
yIn	live (v)
yInroH	life signs (n)
yIntagh	life-support system (n)

yIQ	be wet (v)
yIt	walk (v)
yIv	chew (v)
yIvbeH	tunic (n)
yob	harvest (v)
yoD	shield (n)
yoD	shield (v)
yoH	be brave (v)
yoj	judgment (n)
yol	conflict (n)
yon	be satisfied (v)
yonmoH	satisfy (v)
yong	get in (v)
yopwaH	pants (n)
yoq	humanoid (n)
yoS	district, area (n)
yot	invade (v)
yot	invasion (n)
yotlh	field (of land) (n)
yov	charge (military term) (v)
yoy	be upside down (v)
yo'	fleet (of ships) (n)
yuch	chocolate (n)
yuD	be dishonest (v)
yuDHa'	be honest (v)
yupma'	festival (n)
yuQ	planet (n)
yuQHom	planetoid (n)
yuQjIjQa'	United Federation of Planets (n)
yuv	push (v)
yu'	question, interrogate (v)
yu'egh	wave (n)
'a	but, nevertheless, even so, however (conj)
'ach	but, nevertheless, even so, however (conj)
'aD	vein (n)
'ang	show, reveal (v)
'ar	how many? how much? (ques)
'argh	worsen (v)

115

'av	guard (v)
'avwI'	guard (n)
'aw'	sting (v)
'ay'	section (n)
'eb	opportunity (n)
'eH	ready (excl)
'ej	and (joining sentences) (conj)
'ejDo'	starship, starship class (n)
'ejyo'	Starfleet (n)
'ejyo'waw'	star base (n)
'el	enter, go in (v)
'elaS	Elas (n)
'eng	cloud (n)
'er	type of animal (n)
'et	fore (n)
'etlh	sword (n)
'e'	that (previous topic) (pro)
'IH	be beautiful, handsome (v)
'Ij	listen (v)
'Il	be sincere (v)
'Ip	oath (n)
'Ip	vow, swear (v)
'IQ	be sad (v)
'ISjaH	calendar (n)
'It	be depressed (v)
'Itlh	be advanced, highly developed (v)
'Iv	altitude (n)
'Iv	who? (ques)
'Iw	blood (n)
'och	tunnel (n)
'ogh	invent, devise (v)
'oH	it (pro)
'oj	be thirsty (v)
'ol	verify (v)
'ong	be cunning, sly (v)
'orghen	Organia (n)
'orghen rojmab	Organian Peace Treaty (n)
'orghengan	Organian (n)
'oS	represent (v)
'oSwI'	emissary (n)
'ov	compete (v)

'oy'	ache, hurt, be sore (v)
'oy'	ache, pain, sore (n)
'o'	aft (n)
'ugh	be heavy (v)
'uH	have a hangover, be hung over (v)
'um	be qualified (v)
'uQ	dinner (n)
'urmang	treason (n)
'uS	leg (n)
'ut	be essential, necessary (v)
'utlh	officer (n)
'uy	press down (v)
'uy'	million (num)
'u'	universe (n)

ENGLISH-KLINGON

abandon (v)	lon
ability (n)	laH
above, area above (n)	Dung
absent, be absent (v)	Dach
absentminded, be absent- minded (v)	jeH
abuse (n)	ghong
abuse (v)	ghong
accelerate (v)	chung
accept (v)	laj
acceptance (n)	laj
access (n)	naw'
accidentally, by accident (adv)	bong
accommodate (v)	ma'
accompany (n)	tlhej
accomplish (v)	ta'
accomplished, be accomplished, finished (v)	rIn
accomplishment (n)	ta'
accord (n)	rom
accumulate (v)	vI'
accusation (n)	pum
accuse (v)	pum
ache (n)	'oy'

ache (v)	'oy'
achieve (v)	chav
achievement (n)	chav
acid (n)	pey
acquire (v)	Suq
act, take action (v)	vang
activate (a device) (v)	chu'
add (v)	chel
address, speech, lecture (n)	SoQ
adjust (v)	lIS
administer (v)	loH
administration (n)	loH
admire (v)	Ho'
admit (v)	chID
advance (v)	Duv
advanced, be advanced, highly developed (v)	'Itlh
adversary (n)	ghol
advice (n)	qeS
advise (v)	qeS
aft (n)	'o'
afternoon (n)	pov
agency (n)	tum
agent (n)	Duy
aggressive, be aggressive (v)	vaQ
agonizer, Klingon agonizer (n)	QIghpej
agony (n)	bep
agree (v)	Qochbe'
agriculture (n)	Satlh
aid (v)	QaH
aide (n)	boQ
aide-de-camp (n)	boQDu'
airlock (n)	HIchDal
alarm (n)	ghum
alarm, sound an alarm (v)	ghum
alert (n)	ghuH
alert (v)	ghuHmoH
alerted, be alerted to (v)	ghuH
alien (n)	nov
all (n)	Hoch

all gone, be all gone (v)	loj
alliance (n)	boq
allow (v)	chaw'
alone, be alone (v)	mob
also (conj)	je
alter (v)	choH
altitude (n)	'Iv
always (adv)	reH
ammunition (n)	nIch
analysis (n)	poj
analyze (v)	poj
ancestor (n)	qempa'
ancestors (n)	no'
ancient, be ancient (v)	tIQ
and (joining nouns) (conj)	je
and (joining sentences) (conj)	'ej
anger (n)	QeH
angry, be angry (v)	QeH
animal (n)	Ha'DIbaH
animal: different types of animals (n)	'er, Qogh, Qa'
annoy (v)	nuQ
answer (v)	jang
antimatter (n)	rugh
anyone (n)	vay'
appear (v)	nargh
approach (v)	ghoS
area, district (n)	yoS
argue (v)	ghoH
arm (body part) (n)	DeS
arms (small) (n)	nuHHom
army (n)	mangghom
arrest (v)	qop
arrive (v)	paw
ascend (v)	Sal
ashamed, be ashamed (v)	tuH
ask (v)	tlhob
assemble, meet (v)	ghom
assembly (n)	yej
assist (v)	boQ

asteroid (n)	ghopDap
atmosphere (n)	muD
attack (v)	HIv
attempt (v)	nID
attention, pay attention (v)	qIm
attitude-control thrusters (n)	lolSeHcha
authority (n)	woQ
baby (n)	ghu
back (of body) (n)	Dub
back (of hand) (n)	chap
back away from, back off (v)	DoH
bad, be bad (v)	qab
bandage (n)	Sev
bar, saloon, cocktail lounge (n)	tach
bargain (v)	tlhong
bartender (n)	chom
barter (v)	tlhong
base (military term) (n)	waw'
battle (n)	may'
battle array (n)	may'morgh
battle cruiser (n)	may'Duj
beam (aboard) (v)	jol
beam, transport beam (n)	jol
bear, endure (v)	SIQ
beard (n)	rol
beautiful, be beautiful (v)	'IH
become (v)	moj
beg, plead (v)	qoy'
being (nonhumanoid) (n)	Dep
believe (v)	Har
belly (n)	chor
below, area below (n)	bIng
belt (n)	qogh
bend (v)	SIH
beside, area beside (n)	retlh
betray (v)	magh
between, area between (n)	joj
big, be big (v)	tIn
birthday (n)	qoS

bite (v)	chop
black, be black (v)	qIj
blame (n)	pIch
blame (v)	pIch
block, prevent (v)	bot
blood (n)	'Iw
blow one's top (v)	Qay'
blue, be blue, green, yellow (v)	SuD
board, go aboard (v)	tIj
body (n)	porgh
boil (v)	pub
bold, be bold (v)	jaq
bone (n)	Hom
book (n)	paq
boot (n)	DaS
boot spike (n)	DaSpu'
boring, be boring (v)	Dal
born, be born (v)	bogh
borrow (v)	ngIp
boss (n)	pIn
bother (v)	nuQ
boundary (n)	veH
boy (n)	loDHom
brag (v)	mIy
brain, mind (n)	yab
brave, be brave (v)	yoH
break (v)	ghor
break (rules) (v)	bIv
breakfast (n)	nIQ
breath (n)	tlhuH
breathe (v)	tlhuH
breed (v)	Sep
breeze (n)	SuS
bridge (of a ship) (n)	meH
bright, be bright, light (v)	wov
bring (v)	qem
brother (n)	loDnI'
build up, take form (v)	chen
building (n)	qach
burn (v)	meQ
bury (v)	mol

business (n)	malja'
but (conj)	'ach, 'a
buy (v)	je'
cage (n)	mo'
calculate (v)	SIm
calendar (n)	'ISjaH
call, name (v)	pong
calm, be calm (v)	jot
camp (military term) (n)	raQ
cancel (v)	qIl
cape (clothing) (n)	ngup
capital (of a place) (n)	mon
captain (n)	HoD
capture (v)	jon
care for, take care of (v)	Qorgh
care (about), be concerned (about) (v)	SaH
careful, be careful (v)	yep
careless, be careless (v)	yepHa'
cargo (n)	tep
cargo carrier (n)	tepqengwI'
carry (v)	qeng
catalog (n)	mem
catastrophe (n)	lot
cautious, be cautious (v)	Hoj
cave (n)	DIS
cease, stop (v)	mev
celebrate (v)	lop
center (n)	botlh
certainty (n)	DIch
chain (n)	mIr
chair (n)	quS
change (n)	choH
change (v)	choH
charge (military term) (v)	yov
charge (up) (v)	Huj
charming (used only ironically) (excl)	wejpuH
chase, follow (v)	tlha'
chat (v)	jaw

cheat (v)	ngor
cheek (n)	qevpob
chew (v)	yIv
child, offspring (n)	puq
chin (n)	woS
chocolate (n)	yuch
choice (n)	wIv
choke (v)	voQ
choose (v)	wIv
chore, task (n)	Qu'
chronometer (n)	tlhaq
circle (n)	gho
citizen (n)	rewbe'
city (n)	veng
civilization (n)	tayqeq
civilize (v)	taymoH
civilized, be civilized (v)	tay
claim (territory) (v)	DoQ
classification (n)	buv
classify (v)	buv
clean, be clean (v)	Say'
clear, be clear, not obstructed (v)	Huv
clever, be clever (v)	val
cliff (n)	qoj
climb (v)	toS
clip (v)	poDmoH
clipped, be clipped (v)	poD
cloak, hide (v)	So'
cloaking device (n)	So'wI'
close in, get closer, come nearer (v)	chol
close, shut (v)	SoQmoH
closed, be closed, shut (v)	SoQ
clothing (n)	Sut
cloud (n)	'eng
clumsy, be clumsy (v)	Soy'
coat (n)	wep
cockroach (n)	vetlh
cocktail lounge, bar (n)	tach
code (n)	ngoq
cold, be cold (v)	bIr

collapse (v)	Dej
collar (n)	mongDech
collect (v)	boS
collide (v)	paw'
colony (n)	mID
column (n)	tut
come (v)	ghoS
come on (excl)	Ha'
comet (n)	lIy
command (v)	ra'
commander (n)	la', ra'wI'
commit a crime (v)	HeS
communicate (v)	Qum
communications officer (n)	QumpIn
communicator, communi- cations device (n)	QumwI'
compel (v)	raD
compete (v)	'ov
complain (v)	bep
comply (v)	HeQ
compromise (v)	moS
computer (n)	De'wI'
concentrate (v)	qIm
concentrate on, focus on, think only about (v)	buS
concern, be concerned (about), care (about) (v)	SaH
condemn (v)	qIch
confer (v)	ja'chuq
confess (v)	DIS
confide (v)	tey'
confine (v)	wegh
conflict (n)	yol
confuse (v)	mISmoH
confused, be confused (v)	mIS
confusion (n)	mIS
conglomeration (n)	tlhoQ
congratulate (v)	Hoy'
connect (v)	rar
conquer (v)	chargh

125

consent (v)	ghIb
consequential thing, something important (n)	potlh
conspiracy (n)	QuS
conspire (v)	QuS
consul (n)	jojlu'
contain (an enemy) (v)	Sev
contain (have inside) (v)	ngaS
contradict (v)	tlhoch
contribute (v)	ghaq
control (v)	SeH
control panel (n)	SeHlaw
convey (v)	qeng
convince (v)	pon
cook (v)	vut
cooperate (v)	yeq
coordinates (n)	Quv
corporal (rank) (n)	Da'
corpse (n)	lom
correct, be correct (v)	lugh
corrupt (v)	qalmoH
corrupt, be corrupt (v)	qal
council (n)	yej
Council of Elders (n)	quprIp
count (v)	togh
counterfeit, be counterfeit (v)	ngeb
country, countryside (n)	Hatlh
course, dish (at a meal) (n)	nay'
course, route (n)	He
court (n)	bo'DIj
court-martial (v)	ghIpDIj
coward (n)	nuch
crazy, be crazy (v)	maw'
credit (monetary unit) (n)	DeQ
crew, crewman (n)	beq
crime (n)	HeS
criminal (n)	HeSwI'
crowd (n)	ghom'a'
crowd (v)	qev
cruise (v)	qugh

cry (v)	SaQ
cry out, shout, scream (v)	jach
crystal (geologic formation) (n)	qut
cunning, be cunning (v)	'ong
cure (v)	vor
custom (n)	tIgh
cut (v)	pe'
cut, trim (hair) (v)	chIp
dagger (n)	taj
damage (n)	QIH
damage, cause damage (v)	QIH
dandruff (n)	quHvaj
danger (n)	Qob
dangerous, be dangerous (v)	Qob
dare (v)	ngIl
dark, be dark (v)	Hurgh
data (n)	De'
data transceiving device (n)	HablI'
data transmission (n)	jabbI'ID
daughter (n)	puqbe'
dawn (n)	jajlo'
day (from dawn to dawn) (n)	jaj
day after tomorrow (n)	cha'leS
day before yesterday (n)	cha'Hu'
days ago (n)	Hu'
days from now (n)	leS
daytime (n)	pem
debate (v)	ngach
decay (v)	ragh
deceive (v)	toj
decide (v)	wuq
decline, deteriorate (v)	Sab
decrease (v)	nup
defeat (v)	jey
defect (n)	Duy'
defect (v)	cheH
defective, be defective (n)	Duy'
defend (v)	Hub
defense (n)	Hub

deflectors (n)	begh
delay (v)	mIm
demand (v)	poQ
demolish (v)	pej
Denebia (n)	DenIbya'
Denebian (n)	DenIbya'ngan
Denebian slime devil (n)	DenIbya' Qatlh
deny (v)	tem
deodorant (n)	noSvagh
depart (v)	tlheD
depend on (v)	wuv
depressed, be depressed (v)	'It
descend (v)	ghIr
describe (v)	Del
desert (n)	Deb
desert (v)	choS
deserted, be deserted, empty, uninhabited (v)	chIm
destination (n)	ghoch
destroy (n)	Qaw'
destruction (n)	QIH
deteriorate (v)	Sab
detest (v)	muS
developed, be developed (e.g., civilization) (v)	Hach
device (n)	jan
devise, invent (v)	'ogh
dictator (n)	HI'
dictatorship (n)	HI'tuy
dictionary (n)	mu'ghom
die (v)	Hegh
different, be different (v)	pIm
difficult, be difficult (v)	Qatlh
dignity (n)	nur
dilithium (n)	cha'puj
dilithium crystal (n)	cha'pujqut
dinner (n)	'uQ
diplomacy (n)	ghar
diplomacy, conduct diplomacy (v)	ghar
diplomat (n)	gharwI'
dirt (n)	lam

dirt under fingernails (n)	butlh
dirty, be dirty (v)	lam
disable (v)	Qotlh
disagree (v)	Qoch
disappear (v)	ngab
disaster (n)	Qugh
discipline (n)	Sun
discourage (v)	tung
discover (v)	tu'
discuss (v)	ja'chuq
disease (n)	rop
disgraced, be disgraced (v)	web
disguise (v)	jech
dish, course (food) (n)	nay'
dishonest, be dishonest (v)	yuD
dislike (v)	par
disobey (v)	lobHa'
disperse, scatter (v)	ghomHa'
display, show (picture) (v)	cha'
displeased, be displeased (v)	belHa'
dispute (v)	ghoH
disregard (v)	qImHa'
dissolve (v)	ngoS
distance, range (n)	chuq
distress call (n)	Sotlaw'
distressed, be in distress (v)	Sot
district, area (n)	yoS
distrust (v)	voqHa'
disturb (v)	Suj
divide (v)	wav
dock (n)	vergh
dock (v)	vergh
doctor, physician (n)	Qel
dominate (v)	ghatlh
done (excl)	pItlh
door, gate (n)	lojmIt
doubt (v)	Hon
dread (v)	Haj
dream (v)	naj
dregs (n)	pugh
drill (military) (n)	qeq

drink (v)	tlhutlh
drool (v)	bol
drop (v)	chagh
drunk, be drunk, intoxicated (v)	chech
dry, be dry (v)	QaD
duel (v)	Hay'
dull, be dull, uninteresting (v)	qetlh
dumbfounded, be dumbfounded, shocked (v)	yay'
duty (n)	Qu'
duty station, station (n)	yaH
dysentery (n)	pom
Earth (n)	tera'
Earther, Terran (n)	tera'ngan
earthquake, experience an earthquake or tremor (v)	Qom
easy, be easy (v)	ngeD
eat (v)	Sop
eavesdrop (v)	Daq
edge (n)	HeH
eight (num)	chorgh
eighth (num)	chorghDIch
Elas (n)	'elaS
elder (n)	qup
embark (v)	ten
embassy (n)	rIvSo'
emergency (n)	chach
emissary (n)	Duy, 'oSwI'
emperor (n)	ta', voDleH
empire (n)	wo'
empty, be empty, deserted, uninhabited (v)	chIm
encounter, meet (v)	ghom
encourage (v)	tungHa'
endure, bear (v)	SIQ
enemy (n)	jagh
energize (v)	rIH
energize, fire (e.g., thrusters) (v)	laQ
energizer (n)	rIHwI'

energy beings (n)	HoSDo'
energy field (n)	HoSchem
energy, power (n)	HoS
engage, activate (a device) (v)	chu'
engine (n)	jonta', QuQ
engineer (n)	jonwI'
enjoy (v)	tIv
enough, be enough, be sufficient (v)	yap
enter, go in (v)	'el
entity (n)	Dol
equipment, gear (n)	luch
era (n)	bov
err, make a mistake (v)	Qagh
error, mistake (n)	Qagh
escort (v)	Dor
espionage (n)	lInDab
essential, be essential, necessary (v)	'ut
establish, set up (v)	cher
estimate, judge (v)	noH
ethics (n)	ghob
evade, take evasive action (v)	jun
even so (conj)	'ach, 'a
event, occurrence, phenomenon (n)	wanI'
everyone, everything (n)	Hoch
everywhere (n)	Dat
evil, be evil (v)	mIgh
exact, be exact, perfect (v)	pup
exaggerate (v)	lach
examine (v)	nuD
excellent, be excellent (v)	pov
exceptional, be exceptional, special (v)	le'
exchange, substitute (v)	tam
excite (v)	SeymoH
excited, be excited (v)	Sey
execute, put to death (v)	muH
exhaust (n)	taQbang

exhaust (v)	tlhuch
exile (v)	ghIm
expand (v)	Sach
expect (v)	pIH
expedition (n)	Hoq
experiment (n)	ngong
experiment (v)	ngong
expert, be expert, skilled (v)	po'
explain (v)	QIj
explode (v)	jor
explosive (n)	jorwI'
eye (n)	mIn
eyebrow (n)	Huy'
face (n)	qab
fact (n)	ngoD
factory (n)	laSvargh
fail (v)	luj
fair, be fair (v)	may
faith, have faith in (v)	voq
fake, be fake (v)	ngeb
fall (v)	pum
false, be false (v)	ngeb
family (n)	qorDu'
famous, be famous, well known (v)	noy
fanatical, be fanatical (v)	ngotlh
far, be far, remote (v)	Hop
farm (n)	Du'
farm (v)	wIj
fascinate (v)	vuQ
fast, quickly (adv)	nom
fat, be fat (v)	pI', ror
fatal, be fatal (v)	HeghmoH
fate (n)	San
father (n)	vav
fault (seismic) (n)	Seq
fault, blame (n)	pIch
fed up, be fed up (v)	puQ
Federation (n)	DIvI'
Federation battle cruiser (n)	DIvI'may'Duj

feed (someone else) (v)	je'
feel, touch (v)	Hot
female, woman (n)	be'
festival (n)	yupma'
few, be few, be several, be a handful (v)	puS
fib, lie (v)	nep
field (of land) (n)	yotlh
fierce, be fierce (v)	qu'
fifth (num)	vaghDIch
fight (v)	Suv
fight dirty (v)	HIgh
fill (v)	teb
final, be final, last (v)	Qav
find (v)	tu'
fine, tax (v)	rup
finger (n)	nItlh
finished, be finished, accomplished (v)	rIn
fire (n)	qul
fire (torpedo, rocket, missile) (v)	baH
fire, energize (e.g., thrusters) (v)	laQ
first (num)	wa'DIch
fissure (n)	Qargh
fist (n)	ro'
five (num)	vagh
fix, repair (v)	tI'
flag (n)	joqwI'
flap, flutter, wave (v)	joq
flee, get out (v)	Haw'
fleet (of ships) (n)	yo'
flood (n)	SoD
flood (v)	SoD
floor (n)	rav
flutter, flap, wave (v)	joq
fly (v)	puv
focus on, concentrate on, think only about (v)	buS
follow (a course) (v)	ghoS
follow (rules) (v)	pab

follow, chase (v)	tlha'
fool (n)	qoH
foolish, be foolish, silly (v)	Dogh
foot (n)	qam
forbid (v)	tuch
force (v)	raD
force field (n)	Surchem
fore (n)	'et
forehead (n)	Quch
foreign, be foreign, alien (v)	nov
foreigner (n)	nov
forest, woods (n)	ngem
forget (v)	lIj
fortunate, be fortunate, lucky (v)	Do'
four (num)	loS
fourth (num)	loSDIch
free, be free, independent (v)	tlhab
freedom, independence (n)	tlhab
freeze (v)	taDmoH
freighter (n)	tongDuj
frequency (radio) (n)	Se'
friend (n)	jup
frozen, be frozen (v)	taD
frustrated, be frustrated	mogh
fuel (n)	nIn
function, work, succeed (v)	Qap
funeral (n)	nol
funny, be funny (v)	tlhaQ
galactic rim (n)	qIbHeS
galaxy (n)	qIb
galley (n)	vutpa'
game (n)	Quj
garbage (n)	veQ
garbage scow (n)	veQDuj
gargle (v)	ghagh
gas (n)	SIp
gate (n)	lojmIt
gear, equipment (n)	luch
general (rank) (n)	Sa'

Genesis (n)	qa'vam
genius (n)	wIgh
get (v)	Suq
get away from (v)	DoH
get in (v)	yong
get out, flee (v)	Haw'
get out, take out (v)	lel
get up (v)	Hu'
gift (n)	nob
girl (n)	be'Hom
give (v)	nob
give up, surrender (v)	jegh
glass (tumbler) (n)	HIvje'
glove (n)	pogh
glow (v)	wew
go (v)	jaH
go aboard (v)	tIj
go away from (v)	ghoS
go in (v)	'el
goal (n)	ngoQ
good (expressing satisfaction) (excl)	maj
good, be good (v)	QaQ
good, very good, well done (excl)	majQa'
gossip (v)	joS
gossip, rumor (n)	joS
govern (v)	qum
government (n)	qum
gown (n)	paH
grain (n)	tIr
grammar (n)	pab
grandfather (n)	vavnI'
grandmother (n)	SoSnI'
grave (n)	mol
great, be great, wonderful (v)	Dun
greedy, be greedy (v)	qur
green, be green, blue, yellow (v)	SuD
gripe (v)	bep
grouchy, be grouchy, mean (v)	qej
ground (n)	yav
group (n)	ghom

guard (n)	'avwI'
guard (v)	'av
guess (v)	loy
guest (n)	meb
guide, lead (v)	Dev
guilty, be guilty (v)	DIv
gun, handgun (n)	HIch
gunner (n)	baHwI', matHa'
gunpowder (n)	ngat
hair (on body) (n)	pob
hair (on head) (n)	jIb
half (n)	bID
hand (n)	ghop
handful, be a handful, be few (v)	puS
handgun (n)	HIch
handsome, be handsome (v)	'IH
hang (v)	HuS
hangover, have a hangover, be hung over (v)	'uH
happen, occur (v)	qaS
happy, be happy (v)	Quch
hard, be hard (like a rock) (v)	let
harmful, be harmful (v)	joch
harvest (v)	yob
hassle, be a hassle, be a problem (v)	qay'
hate, detest (v)	muS
have, possess (v)	ghaj
he, she, him, her (pro)	ghaH
head (n)	nach
headache, have a headache (v)	wuQ
healthy, be healthy (v)	pIv
hear (v)	Qoy
heart (n)	tIq
heat (n)	tuj
heavy, be heavy (v)	'ugh
helm (n)	Degh
helmet (n)	mIv

136

helmsman (n)	DeghwI'
help, aid (v)	QaH
her, him, she, he (pro)	ghaH
here, hereabouts (n)	naDev
hide (v)	So'
high, be high (v)	jen
hill, mountain (n)	HuD
him, her, he, she (pro)	ghaH
hinder, interfere (v)	nIS
history (n)	qun
hit (with hand, fist, implement) (v)	qIp
holster (n)	vaH
home (n)	juH
honest, be honest (v)	yuDHa'
honor (n)	batlh
honored, with honor (adv)	batlh
hope (v)	tul
horizontal, be horizontal (v)	SaS
hostage (n)	vub
hot, be hot (v)	tuj
hour (n)	rep
how many? (ques)	'ar
how much? (ques)	'ar
how? (ques)	chay'
however (conj)	'ach, 'a
hull (n)	Som
human (n)	Human
humanoid (n)	yoq
hundred (num)	vatlh
hundred thousand (num)	bIp
hungry, be hungry (v)	ghung
hunt (v)	wam
hurry (v)	moD
hurt (n)	'oy'
hurt (v)	'oy'
husband (n)	loDnal
hypnotize (v)	vong
I, me (pro)	jIH
ice (n)	chuch

idea (n)	qech
identical, be identical (v)	nIb
identify (v)	ngu'
ignorant, be ignorant (v)	jIv
ill, be ill, sick (v)	rop
illegal, be illegal (v)	Hat
immortal, be immortal (v)	jub
impact, strike (v)	mup
impatient, be impatient (v)	boH
important thing, something important (n)	potlh
impressive, be impressive (v)	Doj
improve (v)	Dub
impulse power (n)	Hong
in that case, then, thus, so (adv)	vaj
incompetent, be incompetent (v)	tlhIb
increase (v)	ghur
independence, freedom (n)	tlhab
independent, be independent, free (v)	tlhab
indigestion (n)	poq
infect (v)	ngej
inferior, be inferior (v)	QIv
infirmary (n)	ropyaH
influence (v)	SIgh
information (n)	De'
inhabitant (n)	ngan
inhabited, be inhabited (v)	toq
injure (v)	rIQmoH
injured, be injured (v)	rIQ
innocent, be innocent (v)	chun
insist (v)	qap
instincts (n)	Duj
instruct, teach (v)	ghojmoH
insubordinate, be insubordinate (v)	tlhIv
insult (v)	tIch
insurrection (n)	QuD
intelligent, be intelligent (v)	val
intend, mean to (v)	Hech
intentionally, on purpose (adv)	chIch

interesting, be interesting (v)	Daj
interfere (v)	nIS
interrogate (v)	yu'
interrupt (v)	qagh
intoxicated, be intoxicated, drunk (v)	chech
introduce (v)	lIH
invade (v)	yot
invasion (n)	yot
invent, devise (v)	'ogh
ion (n)	tat
irritable, be irritable (v)	bergh
it (pro)	'oH
jacket, coat (n)	wep
jail (n)	bIghHa'
jog, run (v)	qet
join (v)	muv
journal, log (n)	QonoS
judge, estimate (v)	noH
judgment (n)	yoj
jump (v)	Sup
jurisdiction (n)	teblaw'
just, only, merely (adv)	neH
justice (n)	ruv
keep, save (v)	pol
kellicam (n)	quellI'qam
kevas (n)	qevaS
kick (v)	pup
kidnap (v)	quch
kill (v)	HoH
Klingon (n)	tlhIngan
Klingon Empire (n)	tlhIngan wo'
Klingon writing system (n)	pIqaD
knee (n)	qIv
kneel (v)	tor
knife (n)	taj
know (v)	Sov
label (n)	per

label (v)	per
lake (n)	ngeng
lame, be lame (v)	rIgh
land (n)	puH
land (v)	Saq
landing party (n)	Saqghom
language (n)	Hol
last, be last, final (v)	Qav
lateral, be lateral, move laterally (v)	nech
laugh (v)	Hagh
law (n)	chut
lazy, be lazy (v)	buD
lead, guide (v)	Dev
leak (v)	nIj
learn (v)	ghoj
lecture, speech (n)	SoQ
left (side) (n)	poS
left over, be left over (v)	chuv
leftovers (grammatical term) (n)	chuvmey
leg (n)	'uS
legal, be legal (v)	mub
lend (v)	noj
let's go (excl)	Ha'
lie, fib (v)	nep
lie, recline (v)	Qot
life (n)	yIn
life signs (n)	yInroH
life-support system (n)	yIntagh
light, be light, bright (v)	wov
light (weight), be light (v)	tIS
like (v)	parHa'
limit (v)	vuS
line, rope (n)	tlhegh
lip (n)	wuS
liquor (n)	HIq
listen (v)	'Ij
live (v)	yIn
log, journal (n)	QonoS
long, be long, lengthy (duration) (v)	nI'

long, be long, lengthy (of an object) (v)	tIq
look for, seek, search for (v)	nej
loose, be loose (v)	QeyHa'
loosen (v)	QeyHa'moH
lord (n)	jaw, joH
love, one who is loved (n)	bang
luckily, with luck (adv)	Do'
lucky, be lucky, fortunate (v)	Do'
lunch (n)	megh
machinery (n)	jo', mIqta'
mad, be mad (v)	QeH
maintain (v)	leH
maintenance (n)	leH
male, man (n)	loD
man (n)	loD
manage (v)	vu'
manager (n)	vu'wI'
maneuver (engines) (v)	QoD
maneuver (military term) (n)	tuH
manual, control manually, by hand (v)	ruQ
manuscript (n)	ghItlh
many, be many, numerous (v)	law'
marriage (n)	tlhogh
marry (husband does this) (v)	Saw
marry (wife does this) (v)	nay
matter (n)	Hap
me, I (pro)	jIH
mean, be mean (v)	qej
mean to, intend (v)	Hech
measure (v)	juv
medicine (n)	Hergh
meet (for the first time) (v)	qIH
meet, encounter, assemble (v)	ghom
meeting (n)	qep
melt (v)	tet
memory banks (n)	qawHaq
menu (n)	HIDjolev
merchant (n)	Suy

merchant ship (n)	SuyDuj
mercy (n)	pung
merely, just, only (adv)	neH
messy, be messy, sloppy (v)	ghIH
metal (n)	baS
meteor (n)	chunDab
midday (n)	pemjep
middle, center (n)	botlh
midnight (n)	ramjep
midnight snack (n)	ghem
military (n)	QI'
million (num)	'uy'
mind, brain (n)	yab
mind sifter (Klingon psychic probe) (n)	tuQDoq
mine (v)	tlhIl
miner (n)	tlhIlwI'
mineral (n)	tlhIl
minute (of time) (n)	tup
misinterpret (v)	yajHa'
mission, quest, duty (n)	Qu'
mistake, err, be mistaken, make a mistake (v)	Qagh
mistake, error (n)	Qagh
mix (v)	DuD
mixed up, be mixed up, confused (v)	mIS
module (n)	bobcho'
money (n)	Huch
month (Klingon) (n)	jar
moon (n)	maS
moonlight (n)	maSwov
morning (n)	po
mortal, be mortal (v)	jubbe'
mother (n)	SoS
mountain, hill (n)	HuD
mouth (n)	nuj
mugato (n)	mughato'
murder (v)	chot
muscle (n)	Somraw
mustache (n)	loch

mutiny (v)	qIQ
myth (n)	wIch
nacelle (n)	HanDogh
nag (v)	boj
name (n)	pong
name (v)	pong
nap (v)	Dum
native (n)	Sung
navigate (v)	chIj
navigator (n)	chIjwI'
necessary, be necessary, essential (v)	'ut
neck (n)	mong
necklace (n)	ghIgh
negative (angle), be at a negative angle (v)	taH
negotiate (v)	Sutlh
neighbor (n)	jIl
nervous, be nervous (v)	bIt
Neural (n)	nural
Neuralese (n)	nuralngan
neutral zone (n)	neHmaH
never (adv)	not
nevertheless (conj)	'ach, 'a
new, be new (v)	chu'
next to, area next to (n)	retlh
night (n)	ram
nine (num)	Hut
ninth (num)	HutDIch
no (answer to a question) (excl)	ghobe'
no, I won't, I refuse (excl)	Qo'
nobility (n)	chuQun
noisy, be noisy (v)	chuS
none, nothing (n)	pagh
nonsense (n)	Dap
nose (n)	ghIch
nostril (n)	tlhon
not yet (adv)	wej
nothing, none (n)	pagh
notice (v)	tu'
noun (n)	DIp

nova (n)	puyjaq
now (adv)	DaH
number (n)	mI'
numerous, be numerous (v)	law'
oath (n)	'Ip
obey (v)	lob
object (v)	bep
obliterate (v)	Sang
observe (v)	tu'
obstruct (v)	waQ
obtain (v)	Suq
occupy (military term) (v)	Dan
occur, happen (v)	qaS
occurrence, event, phenomenon (n)	wanI'
ocean (n)	bIQ'a'
odd, be odd (v)	jum
offend (v)	maw
officer (n)	yaS, 'utlh
offspring, child (n)	puq
often (adv)	pIj
okay, yes, I will (excl)	luq, lu'
old, be old (not new) (v)	ngo'
old, be old (not young) (v)	qan
omit (v)	nop
once (adv)	wa'logh
one (num)	wa'
only, merely, just (adv)	neH
onward, go onward, proceed (v)	ghoS
open (v)	poSmoH
open, be open, opened (v)	poS
opinion (n)	vuD
opponent, adversary (n)	ghol
opportunity (n)	'eb
option, possibility (n)	DuH
or, and/or (joining nouns) (conj)	joq
or, and/or (joining sentences) (conj)	qoj
or, either/or (joining nouns) (conj)	ghap

or, either/or (joining sentences) (conj)	pagh
orange, be orange, red (v)	Doq
orbit (v)	bav
order, command (v)	ra'
Organia (n)	'orghenya'
Organian (n)	'orghenya'ngan
Organian Peace Treaty (n)	'orghenya' rojmab
organization (n)	DIvI'
origin (n)	mung
outside (n)	Hur
overhead, area overhead (n)	Dung
override (v)	ngep
overtake, pass (v)	juS
pain (n)	'oy'
pajamas (n)	nIvnav
palm (of hand) (n)	toch
panic (v)	lIm
pants (n)	yopwaH
paper (n)	nav
paper clip (n)	mavjop
parallel, be parallel, go parallel to (v)	Don
parallel course (n)	HeDon
participate (v)	jeS
partner (n)	qoch
party, group (n)	ghom
pass (v)	juS
passenger (n)	raQpo'
passionate, be passionate (v)	nong
patient (n)	SID
patient, be patient (v)	tuv
patrol (v)	ngIv
pay attention (v)	qIm
pause (v)	yev
pay for (v)	DIl
peace (n)	roj
peace, make peace (v)	roj

peace treaty (n)	rojmab
penalty (n)	jIp
percent (n)	vatlhvI'
perfect, be perfect, exact (v)	pup
perhaps (adv)	chaq
permit (n)	chaw'
permit, allow (v)	chaw'
person (humanoid) (n)	ghot, nuv
persuade (v)	pon
pet (n)	Saj
pet, stroke (v)	yach
phaser (n)	pu'
phaser banks (n)	pu'DaH
phaser crew (n)	pu'beq
phaser pistol (n)	pu'HIch
phaser rifle (n)	pu'beH
phenomenon, event, occurrence (n)	wanI'
physician (n)	Qel
pick up (v)	woH
pickle (cucumber) (n)	Hurgh
pity (v)	vup
place (v)	lan
plan (v)	nab
planet (n)	yuQ
planetoid (n)	yuQHom
plant (v)	poch
plastic (n)	mep
play (v)	reH
play a game (v)	Quj
plead, beg (v)	qoy'
pleased, be pleased (v)	bel
pleasure (n)	bel
poison (n)	tar
ponytail (n)	DaQ
ponytail holder (n)	choljaH
popular, be popular (v)	Qat
population (n)	roghvaH
possess, have (v)	ghaj
possibility, option (n)	DuH
possible, be possible (v)	DuH

postpone (v)	lum
power (political) (n)	woQ
power, energy (n)	HoS
powerful, be powerful (v)	HoSghaj
practice, train, prepare (v)	qeq
precede (v)	nung
predecessor (n)	nubwI'
prefer (v)	maS
prefix (n)	moHaq
prepare for, be alerted to (v)	ghuH
prepare, train, practice (v)	qeq
prepared, be prepared (to launch) (v)	ghuS
present (v)	much
present, be present (not absent) (v)	SaH
presentation (n)	much
preserve (v)	choq
press down (v)	'uy
prevent, block (v)	bot
primitive, be primitive (v)	lutlh
prison, jail (n)	bIghHa'
prisoner (n)	qama'
privilege (n)	DIb
prize (n)	tev
problem, be a problem, be a hassle (v)	qay'
proceed on a course, go onward (v)	ghoS
proclaim (v)	maq
procrastinate (v)	lum
produce (v)	lIng
program (a computer) (v)	ghun
progress (n)	Ser
progress (v)	tlhetlh
prohibit (v)	bot
project (n)	jInmol
project, put on (screen) (v)	Hotlh
promise (v)	lay'
promote (v)	num
propel (v)	vo'

prosper, be prosperous (v)	chep
protect (v)	Qan
proud, be proud (v)	Hem
prove (v)	tob
punish (v)	Hup
pupil (of eye) (n)	lur
purchase (v)	je'
pure, be pure (v)	watlh
purposely, on purpose, intentionally (adv)	chIch
push (v)	yuv
put down (v)	roQ
put on (clothes) (v)	tuQmoH
put on (screen), project (v)	Hotlh
putrid, be putrid (v)	ngIm
quadrotriticale (n)	loSpev
qualified, be qualified (v)	'um
quarrel (v)	Sol
quest (n)	Qu'
question, interrogate (v)	yu'
quickly (adv)	nom
quiet, be quiet (v)	tam
quit (v)	bup
race (type, sort, class) (n)	Segh
radan (crude dilithium crystal) (n)	Dom
raid (v)	weH
rain (v)	SIS
raise (v)	pep
range, distance (n)	chuq
ransom (n)	voHDajbo'
rare, be rare (v)	qub
raw, be raw, unprocessed (v)	tlhol
ray (n)	tIH
reach (v)	SIch
read (v)	laD
ready (excl)	'eH
ready, standing by (excl)	SuH, Su'
realize (v)	tlhoj

reason (n)	meq
reason (v)	meq
rebel (n)	lotlhwI'
rebel (v)	lotlh
receive (v)	Hev
recline, lie (v)	Qot
recognize (v)	ghov
recommend, suggest (v)	chup
record (n)	ta
record (v)	qon
red, be red, orange (v)	Doq
refuge (n)	lulIgh
refuse, I refuse (excl)	Qo'
region (n)	Sep
regret (v)	pay
Regulan (n)	reghuluSngan
Regulan bloodworm (n)	reghuluS 'Iwghargh
Regulus (n)	reghuluS
reign, rule (v)	che'
relax, rest (v)	leS
relieve (v)	Son
religion (n)	lalDan
rely on (v)	wuv
remain (v)	ratlh
remember (v)	qaw
remind (v)	qawmoH
remote, be remote, far (v)	Hop
remove, take off (v)	teq
Remus (n)	rIymuS
rendezvous (v)	ghom
repair (v)	tI'
reply (v)	jang
report, tell (v)	ja'
represent (v)	'oS
require (v)	poQ
rescue (v)	toD
research (v)	Qul
resemble (v)	rur
resent (v)	qeH
resign (v)	paj
resource (n)	Sup

resources (n)	jo
respect (v)	vuv
responsible, be responsible (v)	ngoy'
rest, relax (v)	leS
restaurant (n)	Qe'
restless, be restless (v)	ngoj
retaliate (v)	noD
retreat (v)	HeD
return (v)	chegh
reveal, show (v)	'ang
revenge (n)	bortaS
revolt (v)	Daw'
revolt, revolution (n)	Daw'
rich, be rich (v)	mIp
ride (v)	lIgh
ridicule (v)	nuS
rifle (n)	beH
right (side) (n)	nIH
right, be right, correct (v)	lugh
ring (for finger) (n)	Qeb
river (n)	bIQtIq
roam, travel, rove (v)	leng
rob (v)	Hej
robe (n)	mop
robot (n)	qoq
rock, stone (n)	nagh
Romulan (n)	romuluSngan
Romulus (n)	romuluS
room (n)	pa'
rope, line (n)	tlhegh
rotten, be rotten (v)	non
rough, be rough (v)	ghegh
round up (v)	lIq
route, course (n)	He
rove, roam, travel (v)	leng
rover (grammatical term) (n)	lengwI'
rude, be rude (v)	Doch
ruins (n)	pIgh
rule, reign, run (v)	che'
rumor, gossip (n)	joS
run, jog (v)	qet

run, rule (v)	che'
ruthless, be ruthless (v)	wIH
sabotage (v)	Sorgh
saccharin (n)	HaQchor
sad, be sad (v)	'IQ
saloon, bar (n)	tach
salute (v)	van
same, be the same (v)	rap
satellite (n)	SIbDoH
satisfied, be satisfied (v)	yon
satisfy (v)	yonmoH
save, keep (v)	pol
save, rescue (v)	toD
scan (v)	Hotlh
scanner (n)	HotlhwI'
scare (v)	ghIj
scatter, disperse (v)	ghomHa'
scavenge (v)	qor
school (n)	DuSaQ
science (n)	QeD
science officer (n)	QeDpIn
scientist (n)	tej
scold (v)	qun
scream, cry out, shout (v)	jach
screen, viewing screen (n)	jIH
search for, seek, look for (v)	nej
second (num)	cha'DIch
second (of time) (n)	lup
secret (n)	pegh
secret, keep something secret (v)	pegh
section (n)	'ay'
sector, zone (n)	mIch
security (n)	Hung
see (v)	legh
seek, search for (v)	nej
select (v)	wIv
self-confident, be self-confident (v)	jeQ
selfish, be selfish (v)	mut
sell (v)	ngev
send (v)	ngeH

sensor (n)	noch
sentence (n)	mu'tlhegh
separate (v)	chev
sergeant (n)	bu'
serious, be serious (v)	Sagh
serpent, worm (n)	ghargh
servant (n)	toy'wI'
serve (a master) (v)	toy'
serve (food) (v)	jab
set up, establish (v)	cher
seven (num)	Soch
seventh (num)	SochDIch
several, be several (v)	puS
shadow (n)	QIb
shame (v)	tuHmoH
sharp, be sharp (v)	jej
she, he, her, him (pro)	ghaH
Sherman's Planet (n)	SermanyuQ
shield (n)	yoD
shield (v)	yoD
shine, be shiny (v)	boch
ship, vessel (n)	Duj
shocked, be shocked, dumbfounded (v)	yay'
shoe (n)	waq
shoot (v)	bach
shore leave (n)	leSpoH
shortcut (n)	qIgh
shot (n)	bach
shoulder (n)	volchaH
shout, scream, cry out (v)	jach
show, display (picture) (v)	cha'
show, reveal (v)	'ang
shut (v)	SoQmoH
shut, be shut (v)	SoQ
sick, be sick, ill (v)	rop
side (n)	Dop
sight (with gunsight) (v)	puS
sign (a treaty) (v)	qI'
silence (v)	tammoH
silly, be silly (v)	Dogh

simple, be simple (v)	nap
simultaneous, happen simultaneously (v)	quq
sin (v)	yem
sincere, be sincere (v)	'Il
sir (n)	qaH
sister (n)	be'nI'
sit (v)	ba'
situation (n)	ghu'
six (num)	jav
sixth (num)	javDIch
skilled, be skilled (v)	po'
skin (n)	DIr
skin (v)	Surgh
sky (n)	chal
sleep (v)	Qong
slightly, a little bit (adv)	loQ
slingshot (n)	moy'bI'
slit (v)	SIj
sloppy, be sloppy, messy (v)	ghIH
slowly (adv)	QIt
sly, be sly (v)	'ong
small, be small (v)	mach
smart, be smart (v)	val
smear (v)	ngoH
smell, emit odor (v)	He'
smell, sense odors (v)	largh
smoke (n)	tlhIch
smooth, be smooth (v)	Hab
snow (v)	peD
so, then, thus, in that case (adv)	vaj
so, well (excl)	toH
society (n)	nugh
socks (n)	paSlogh
soft, be soft (v)	tun
soldier (n)	mang
soldiers (n)	negh
solid, be solid (v)	Sub
solution (liquid) (n)	taS
somebody, something, anybody, anything (n)	vay'

sometimes (adv)	rut
somewhere (n)	vogh
son (n)	puqloD
soon (adv)	tugh
sore (n)	'oy'
sore, be sore (v)	'oy'
sorry, be sorry (v)	QoS
sour, be sour (v)	wIb
source (n)	Hal
space (n)	logh
space station (n)	tengchaH
speak (v)	jatlh
special, be special, exceptional (v)	le'
species (n)	mut
specimen (n)	chovnatlh
speech (vocal sounds) (n)	QIch
speech, lecture, address (n)	SoQ
sphere (n)	moQ
spin (v)	DIng
spine (n)	pIp
spy (n)	ghoqwI'
spy (v)	ghoq
squadron (n)	nawlogh
stab (v)	DuQ
stand (v)	Qam
standing by, ready (excl)	SuH, Su'
star (n)	Hov
star base (n)	'ejyo'waw'
star system (n)	Hovtay'
Starfleet (n)	'ejyo'
starship, starship class (n)	'ejDo'
station, duty station (n)	yaH
status (n)	Dotlh
steal (v)	nIH
steam (n)	SeS
step on (v)	gho'
sticky, be sticky (v)	Hum
sting (v)	'aw'
stink (v)	He'So'
stomach (n)	burgh
stone, rock (n)	nagh

stoop (v)	joD
stop, cease (v)	mev
storm (v)	jev
story (n)	lut
strange, be strange (v)	Huj
strategy (n)	Dup
strength (n)	HoS
strike, impact (v)	mup
stroke, pet (v)	yach
strong, be strong (v)	HoS
structure, building (n)	qach
stubborn, be stubborn (v)	mul
student (n)	ghojwI'
study (v)	HaD
stuff (v)	ghoD
stupid, be stupid (v)	QIp
sublight speed (n)	gho'Do
substitute (v)	tam
succeed, work, function (v)	Qap
success (n)	Qapla'
suddenly (adv)	pay'
suffer (v)	bech
sufficient, be sufficient (v)	yap
suffix (n)	mojaQ
suggest, recommend (v)	chup
suicide, commit suicide (v)	HoH'egh
superior (n)	moch
superior, be superior (v)	nIv
support (military term) (n)	ngaq
surface (of a planet) (n)	ghor
surgery (n)	Haq
surprise (v)	mer
surrender, give up (v)	jegh
surround (v)	Dech
suspect, be suspect (v)	nub
suspicious, be suspicious (v)	pIH
swallow (v)	ghup
swear, vow (v)	'Ip
switch (n)	leQ
sword (n)	'etlh
system (n)	pat

155

tactical display (n)	wIy
tactical officer (n)	ya
tactics (n)	to'
take (v)	tlhap
take action (v)	vang
take away (v)	nge'
take care of, care for (v)	Qorgh
take down (v)	jotlh
take form, build up (v)	chen
take off, remove (v)	teq
take out, get out (v)	lel
target (n)	DoS
targets (n)	ray'
task, chore (n)	Qu'
tax (v)	rup
teach, instruct (v)	ghojmoH
teachings (n)	paQDI'norgh
technician (n)	chamwI'
tell, report (v)	ja'
Tellun Star System (n)	telun Hovtay'
temperature (n)	Hat
temple (structure) (n)	chIrgh
temporary, be temporary (v)	ru'
tempt (v)	tlhu'moH
tempted, be tempted (v)	tlhu'
ten (combining form) (num)	maH
ten (num)	wa'maH
ten thousand (num)	netlh
tenth (num)	wa'maHDIch
Terran (n)	tera'ngan
that (previous topic) (pro)	'e', net
them, they (capable of using language) (pro)	chaH
them, they (incapable of language) (pro)	bIH
then, thus, in that case, so (adv)	vaj
theory (n)	nger
theragen (n)	Qab
there, over there, thereabouts (n)	pa'
they, them (capable of using language) (pro)	chaH

they, them (incapable of language) (pro)	bIH
thief (n)	nIHwI'
thin, be thin (v)	lang
thing (n)	Doch
think (v)	Qub
think only about, concentrate on, focus on (v)	buS
third (num)	wejDIch
thirsty, be thirsty (v)	'oj
thousand (num)	SaD, SanID
threaten (v)	buQ
three (num)	wej
throat (n)	Hugh
throw away (v)	woD
thrust (v)	ghoS
thruster (n)	vIj
thrusters (n)	chuyDaH
thus, so, in that case (adv)	vaj
tickle (v)	qotlh
tight, be tight (v)	Qey
tighten (v)	QeymoH
time (v)	poH
time, period of time (n)	poH
tired, be tired (v)	Doy'
toe (n)	yaD
together, be together (v)	tay'
toilet (n)	puch
tolerate (v)	chergh
tomorrow (n)	wa'leS
tongue (n)	jat
tooth (n)	Ho'
toothache (n)	Ho''oy'
topaline (n)	toplIn
torpedo (n)	peng
torpedoes (n)	cha
torpedo tube (n)	chetvI', DuS
torture (v)	joy'
touch, feel (v)	Hot
tough, be tough (v)	rotlh
toxic, be toxic (v)	SuQ

trade (v)	mech
tradition (n)	lurDech
train, prepare (v)	qeq
traitor (n)	maghwI'
transact (v)	Huq
transceiving device (for data) (n)	HablI'
transfer (v)	Qay
translate (v)	mugh
translator (n)	mughwI'
transmission (of data) (n)	jabbI'ID
transmit data (to a place) (v)	lI'
transmit data (away from a place) (v)	lab
transport (v)	lup
transport beam (n)	jol
transport room (n)	jolpa'
transporter ionizer unit (n)	jolvoy'
travel, roam (v)	leng
treason (n)	'urmang
treaty (n)	mab
tree (n)	Sor
tremor, experience a tremor (v)	Qom
tribble (n)	yIH
trick (v)	toj
tricorder (n)	Hoqra'
trifling, be trifling, trivial, unimportant (v)	ram
trillium (n)	DIlyum
trim (hair) (v)	chIp
trip (n)	leng
triumph, victory (n)	yay
trivial, be trivial, trifling, unimportant (v)	ram
troops (n)	QaS
trouble (n)	Seng
trouble, cause trouble (v)	Seng
Troyius (n)	Doy'yuS
truce (n)	rojHom
true, be true (v)	teH
trunk (of body) (n)	ro
trust, have faith in (v)	voq
truth, tell the truth (v)	vIt

try (v)	nID
tube, torpedo tube (n)	chetvI', DuS
tunic (n)	yIvbeH
tunnel (n)	'och
turn (v)	tlhe'
twice (adv)	cha'logh
twilight (n)	choS
two (num)	cha'
ugly, be ugly (v)	moH
unconditional surrender (n)	Doghjey
unconscious, be unconscious (v)	vul
under, area under (n)	bIng
underground (n)	wutlh
understand (v)	yaj
undress (v)	tuQHa'moH
uneasy, be uneasy (v)	bIt, jotHa'
unhappy, be unhappy (v)	QuchHa'
uniform (n)	HIp
unimportant, be unimportant, trivial (v)	ram
uninhabited, be uninhabited, empty, deserted (v)	chIm
uninteresting, be uninteresting (v)	qetlh
United Federation of Planets (n)	yuQjIjDIvI'
universe (n)	'u'
unprocessed, be unprocessed, raw (v)	tlhol
unusual, be unusual (v)	motlhbe'
upside down, be upside down (v)	yoy
urgent, be urgent (v)	pav
us, we (pro)	maH
use (v)	lo'
useful, be useful (v)	lI'
usual, be usual (v)	motlh
vacate (v)	qeD
vacation, take a vacation (v)	ghIQ
valley (n)	ngech
valuable, be valuable (v)	lo'laH
vanish (v)	ngab
variety (n)	Sar

various, be varied (v)	Sar
vegetation (n)	tI
vein (n)	'aD
velocity (n)	Do
vent (n)	yIb
verb (n)	wot
verify (v)	'ol
vertical, be vertical (v)	chong
vessel, ship (n)	Duj
vicious, be vicious (v)	naS
victory, triumph (n)	yay
viewing screen (n)	jIH
violent, be violent (v)	ral
visit (v)	Such
visual display (n)	HaSta
vocabulary (n)	mu'tay'
voice (n)	ghogh
volunteer (v)	Sap
vow, swear (v)	'Ip
voyage (n)	leng
Vulcan (person) (n)	vulqangan
Vulcan (planet) (n)	vulqan
vulgar, be vulgar (v)	Qut
wait (for) (v)	loS
wake (someone) up (v)	vemmoH
wake up, cease sleeping (v)	vem
walk (v)	yIt
want (v)	neH
war (n)	veS
warn (n)	ghuHmoH
warp drive (n)	pIvghor
washroom (n)	puchpa'
watch (v)	bej
water (n)	bIQ
wave, flap, flutter (v)	joq
we, us (pro)	maH
weak, be weak (v)	puj
weapon (n)	nuH
wear (clothes) (v)	tuQ
week (Klingon) (n)	Hogh

well done, very good (excl)	majQa'
well, so (excl)	toH
what do you want? (greeting) (excl)	nuqneH
what? (ques)	nuq
when? (ques)	ghorgh
where? (ques)	nuqDaq
white, be white (v)	chIS
who? (ques)	'Iv
why? (ques)	qatlh
wife (n)	be'nal
wind, breeze (n)	SuS
woman (n)	be'
won't, I won't, I refuse (excl)	Qo'
wonderful, be wonderful, great (v)	Dun
woods, forest (n)	ngem
word (n)	mu'
work, function (v)	Qap
work, toil (v)	vum
worm, serpent (n)	ghargh
worsen (v)	'argh
worthless, be worthless (v)	lo'laHbe'
write (v)	ghItlh
writing system, Klingon writing system (n)	pIqaD
yawn (v)	Hob
year (Klingon) (n)	DIS
years ago (n)	ben
years from now (n)	nem
yellow, be yellow, blue, green (v)	SuD
yes, okay, I will (excl)	luq, lu'
yes, true (answer to yes/no question) (excl)	HIja', HISlaH
yesterday (n)	wa'Hu'
you (plural) (pro)	tlhIH
you (pro)	SoH
young, be young (v)	Qup
zero (num)	pagh
zone, sector (n)	mIch

KLINGON AFFIXES

1. Noun suffixes

Numbers indicate suffix type.

-chaj	4	their
-Daj	4	his/her
-Daq	5	locative
-Du'	2	plural (body part)
-Hey	3	apparent
-Hom	1	diminutive
-lIj	4	your
-lI'	4	your (noun capable of using language)
-maj	4	our
-ma'	4	our (noun capable of using language)
-mey	2	plural (general)
-mo'	5	due to
-na'	3	definite
-pu'	2	plural (beings capable of using language)
-qoq	3	so-called
-raj	4	your (plural)
-ra'	4	your (plural) (noun capable of using language)
-vaD	5	for
-vam	4	this

-vetlh	4	that
-vo'	5	from
-wIj	4	my
-wI'	4	my (noun capable of using language)
-'a'	1	augmentative
-'e'	5	topic

2. Pronominal prefixes

0	he/she/it (no object), he/she/it–him/her/it/them, they (no object), they–them
bI-	you (no object)
bo-	you (plural)–him/her/it/them
che-	you (plural)–us
cho-	you–me
Da-	you–him/her/it/them
DI-	we–them
Du-	he/she/it–you
gho-	imperative: you–us, you (plural)–us
HI-	imperative: you–me, you (plural)–me
jI-	I (no object)
ju-	you–us
lI-	he/she/it–you (plural), they–you (plural)
lu-	they–him/her/it
ma-	we (no object)
mu-	he/she/it–me, they–me
nI-	they–you
nu-	he/she/it–us, they–us
pe-	imperative: you (plural) (no object)
pI-	we–you
qa-	I–you
re-	we–you (plural)
Sa-	I–you (plural)
Su-	you (plural) (no object)
tI-	imperative: you–them, you (plural)–them
tu-	you (plural)–me
vI-	I–him/her/it/them
wI-	we–him/her/it
yI-	imperative: you (no object), you–him/her/it, you (plural)–him/her/it

3. Verb suffixes

Numbers indicate suffix type; R stands for rover.

-beH	2	ready, set up (referring to devices)
-bej	6	certainly, undoubtedly
-be'	R	not
-bogh	9	which (relative-clause marker)
-choH	3	change
-chugh	9	if
-chuq	1	one another
-chu'	6	clearly, perfectly
-DI'	9	as soon as, when
-Ha'	R	undo
-laH	5	can, able
-law'	6	seems, apparently
-lI'	7	in progress
-lu'	5	indefinite subject
-meH	9	for (purpose-clause marker)
-moH	4	cause
-neS	8	honorific
-nIS	2	need
-pa'	9	before
-pu'	7	perfective
-qang	2	willing
-qa'	3	do again, resume
-qu'	R	emphatic
-Qo'	R	don't!, won't
-rup	2	ready, prepared (referring to beings)
-taH	7	continuous
-ta'	7	accomplished, done
-vIp	2	afraid
-vIS	9	while
-wI'	9	one who is, one who does, thing which does
-'a'	9	interrogative
-'egh	1	oneself

4. Special number suffixes

-DIch	forms ordinal numbers (*first, second,* etc.)
-logh	forms *once, twice, three times,* etc.

ENGLISH INDEX TO KLINGON AFFIXES

1. Noun suffixes

Numbers indicate suffix type.

apparent	-Hey	3
augmentative	-'a'	1
definite	-na'	3
diminutive	-Hom	1
due to	-mo'	5
for	-vaD	5
from	-vo'	5
his/her	-Daj	4
locative	-Daq	5
my	-wIj	4
my (noun capable of using language)	-wI'	4
our	-maj	4
our (noun capable of using language)	-ma'	4
plural (beings capable of using language)	-pu'	2
plural (body part)	-Du'	2
plural (general)	-mey	2
so-called	-qoq	3
that	-vetlh	4
their	-chaj	4
this	-vam	4

topic	-'e'	5
your	-lIj	4
your (noun capable of using language)	-lI'	4
your (plural)	-raj	4
your (plural) (noun capable of using language)	-ra'	4

2. Pronominal prefixes

he/she/it (no object)	0
he/she/it–him/her/it/them	0
he/she/it–me	mu-
he/she/it–us	nu-
he/she/it–you	Du-
he/she/it–you (plural)	lI-
I (no object)	jI-
I–him/her/it/them	vI-
I–you	qa-
I–you (plural)	Sa-
they (no object)	0
they–him/her/it	lu-
they–me	mu-
they–them	0
they–us	nu-
they–you	nI-
they–you (plural)	lI-
we (no object)	ma-
we–him/her/it	wI-
we–them	DI-
we–you	pI-
we–you (plural)	re-
you (no object)	bI-
you–him/her/it/them	Da-
you–me	cho-
you–us	ju-
you (plural) (no object)	Su-
you (plural)–him/her/it/them	bo-
you (plural)–me	tu-
you (plural)–us	che-
imperative: you (no object)	yI-
imperative: you–him/her/it	yI-

imperative: you–me	HI-
imperative: you–them	tI-
imperative: you–us	gho-
imperative: you (plural) (no object)	pe-
imperative: you (plural)–him/her/it	yI-
imperative: you (plural)–me	HI-
imperative: you (plural)–them	tI-
imperative: you (plural)–us	gho-

3. Verb suffixes

Numbers indicate suffix type; R stands for rover.

able	-laH	5
accomplished	-ta'	7
afraid	-vIp	2
apparently	-law'	6
as soon as	-DI'	9
before	-pa'	9
can	-laH	5
cause	-moH	4
certainly	-bej	6
change	-choH	3
clearly	-chu'	6
continuous	-taH	7
do again	-qa'	3
don't!	-Qo'	R
done	-ta'	7
emphatic	-qu'	R
for (purpose-clause marker)	-meH	9
honorific	-neS	8
if	-chugh	9
in progress	-lI'	7
indefinite subject	-lu'	5
interrogative	-'a'	9
need	-nIS	2
not	-be'	R
one another	-chuq	1
one who is, one who does	-wI'	9
oneself	-'egh	1
perfective	-pu'	7

perfectly	-chu'	6
prepared (referring to beings)	-rup	2
progress, in progress	-lI'	7
ready (referring to beings)	-rup	2
ready (referring to devices)	-beH	2
resume	-qa'	3
seems	-law'	6
set up (referring to devices)	-beH	2
thing which is, thing which does	-wI'	9
undo	-Ha'	R
undoubtedly	-bej	6
when	-DI'	9
which (relative-clause marker)	-bogh	9
while	-vIS	9
willing	-qang	2
won't	-Qo'	R

4. Special number suffixes

ordinal numbers (*first, second,* etc.)	-DIch
once, twice, three times, etc.	-logh

APPENDIX

A Selected List of Useful Klingon Expressions

For those who want to make an attempt at speaking Klingon without reading the grammatical description of the language, a rough pronunciation for each expression is given as a guide. The letters can be read with their normal English values, with the following special conventions:

a	as in	*pa*
e	as in	*pet*
i	as in	*pit*
o	as in	*go*
oo	as in	*soon*
ow	as in	*cow*
y	as in	*cry (when used as a vowel)*
kh	as *ch* in German *Bach* or Scottish *loch*	
gh	as a softer *kh*, with humming (or voicing) at the same time	

In words of more than one syllable, stressed syllables are written in all capital letters.

Those who follow the rough pronunciation without learning the proper Klingon pronunciation described in section 1 of this dictionary should be aware that they will be speaking with a strong Terran accent.

APPENDIX

ENGLISH	KLINGON	ROUGH PRONUNCIATION
Yes.	HIja' *or* HISlaH	khi-JA *or* khish-LAKH
No.	ghobe'	gho-BE
I've done it! I've finished!	pItlh	pitl
Well! Aha!	toH	tokh
How did this happen? What's going on?	chay'	chy
I don't understand.	jIyajbe'	ji-YAJ-be
I don't care.	jISaHbe'	ji-SHAKH-be
No problem!	qay'be'	ky-BE
Do you speak Klingon?	tlhIngan Hol Dajatlh'a'	TLIngan khol da-jatl-A
I cannot speak Klingon.	tlhIngan Hol vIjatlhlaHbe'	TLIngan khol vi-JATL-lakh-BE
Where is a good restaurant?	nuqDaq 'oH Qe' QaQ'e'	NOOK-dak okh kkhe KKHAKKH-e
Where is the bathroom?	nuqDaq 'oH puchpa''e'	NOOK-dak okh pooch-PA-e
How much fuel do we have left?	nIn 'ar wIghaj	nin ar wi-GHAJ
I won't (do it)!	Qo'	kkho
Feed him!	yIje'	yi-JE
You are right.	bIlugh	bi-LOOGH
You are wrong.	bIlughbe'	bi-loogh-BE
Am I disturbing you?	qaSuj'a'	ka-shooj-A
It's not my fault.	pIch vIghajbe'	pich vi-ghaj-BE
My chronometer has stopped.	tlhaqwIj chu'Ha'lu'pu'	TLAK-wij choo-KHA-loo-poo
The engine is overheating.	tujqu'choH QuQ	tooj-KOO-chokh kkhookkh
Where can I get my shoes cleaned?	nuqDaq waqwIj vIllamHa'choHmoH	NOOK-dak WAK-wij vi-lam-KHA-chokh-mokh
Will it hurt?	'oy''a'	oy-A
Beam me aboard.	HIjol	khi-JOL
Activate the transport beam!	jol yIchu'	jol yi-CHOO
Surrender or die!	bIjeghbe'chugh vaj bIHegh	bi-jegh-BE-choogh vaj bi-KHEGH
We will meet in the cocktail lounge.	tachDaq maghom	TACH-dak ma-GHOM
Your nose is shiny.	boch ghIchraj	boch GHICH-raj

USEFUL KLINGON EXPRESSIONS

English	Klingon	Pronunciation
Always trust your instincts.	Duj tlvoqtaH	dooj ti-VOK-takh
There are Klingons around here.	naDev tlhInganpu' tu'lu'	na-DEV tlingan-POO TOO-loo
Don't tell him/her!	ylja'Qo'	yi-ja-KKHO
Come here!	HIghoS	khi-GHOSH
Go to jail.	bIghHa'Daq ylghoS	bigh-KHA-dak yi-GHOSH
Put him on screen.	ylHotlh	yi-KHOTL
That is unfortunate.	Do'Ha'	do-KHA
Understood. I understand.	jIyaj	ji-YAJ
Success!	Qapla'	kkhap-LA
You will be remembered with honor.	batlh DaqawluʼtaH	batl da-KOW-loo-takh
Animal!	Ha'DIbaH	KHA-di-bakh
There's nothing happening here.	naDev qaS wanI' ramqu'	na-DEV kash wa-NI ram-KOO
(Is that) understood?	yaj'a'	yaj-A
Your ship is a garbage scow.	veQDuj 'oH DujllIʼe'	vekkh-DOOJ okh DOOJ-lij-E
I have a headache.	jIwuQ	ji-WOOKKH
Hurry up!	tugh	toogh
Very good! Well done!	majQa'	maj-KKHA
What do you want? (greeting)	nuqneH	nook-NEKH
Okay.	lu' or luq	loo or look
When will the water be hot?	ghorgh tujchoHpu' bIQ	ghorgh TOOJ-chokh-poo bikkh
Is this seat taken?	quSDaq ba' lu''a'	KOOSH-dak BA-loo-a
I can't find my communicator.	Qumwl'wlj vltu'laHbe'	kkhoom-WI-wij vi-TOO-lakh-BE
This helmet suits you.	Du'IHchoHmoH mIvvam	doo-IKH-chokh-mokh MIV-vam
You need a rest.	bIleSnIS	bi-LESH-nish
Pay now!	DaH ylDIl	dakh yi-DIL
Four thousand throats may be cut in one night by a running man.	qaStaHvIS wa' ram loS SaD Hugh SIjlaH qetbogh loD	KASH-takh-vish wa ram losh shad khoogh SHIJ-lakh KET-bogh lod
Revenge is a dish which is best served cold.	bortaS bIr jablu'DI'reH QaQqu' nay'	bor-TASH bir JAB-loo-DI rekh kkhakkh-KOO ny
How much do you want for that?	Dochvetlh DIlmeH Huch 'ar DaneH	DOCH-vetl DIL-mekh khooch ar da-NEKH

171

APPENDIX

I'm lost.	iIHtaHbogh naDev vISovbe'	JIKH-takh-bogh na-DEV vi-shov-BE
I can't eat that.	Dochvetlh vISoplaHbe'	DOCH-vetl vi-SHOP-lakh-BE
I can't drink that.	Dochvetlh vItlhutlhlaHbe'	DOCH-vetl vi-TLOOTL-lakh-BE
Go away!	naDev vo' yIghoS	na-dev-VO yi-GHOSH
What do I do with this? (i.e., How do I use this?)	chay' Dochvam vIlo'	chy DOCH-vam vi-LO
What do I do with this? (i.e., Where do I put this?)	nuqDaq Dochvam vIlan	NOOK-dak DOCH-vam vi-LAN
I've never seen him/her before.	not vIleghpu'	not vi-LEGH-poo
I didn't do it.	vIta'pu'be'	vi-TA-poo-BE
I wasn't there.	pa' jIHpu'be'	pa JIKH-poo-BE
You look terrible. (i.e., You seem unhealthy.)	bIpIvHa'law'	bi-piv-KHA-low
You look terrible. (i.e., You're very ugly.)	bImoHqu'	bi-mokh-KOO
You lie.	bInep	bi-NEP
Be quiet! (i.e., Become quiet!)	yItamchoH	yi-TAM-chokh
Be quiet! (i.e., Don't speak!)	yIjatlhQo'	yi-jatl-KKHO
Shut up! (i.e., Stop speaking!)	bIjatlh 'e' yImev	bi-JATL e yi-MEV
Where do I sleep?	nuqDaq jIQong	NOOK-dak ji-KKHONG
Does it bite?	chop'a'	chop-A
Will you read my manuscript?	ghItlh vIghItlhta'bogh DalaD'a'	ghitl vi-GHITL-ta-bogh da-lad-A
Where do you keep the chocolate?	nuqDaq yuch Dapol	NOOK-dak yooch da-POL

172

INTRODUCTION TO THE ADDENDUM

The original edition of this dictionary was never intended to contain a complete description of the Klingon language, but only an outline of some of its more important grammatical features and a representative sample of its vocabulary. Since its appearance, study of the language has continued and a great deal more has been learned. Unfortunately, due to a number of factors, including the recession currently affecting most of this sector as well as recent political changes, research funds have become more difficult to come by, delaying the completion of analysis of the language. Indeed, work has been stalled on a number of worthwhile projects, including the *Klingon Encyclopedia* and the *Romulan Chrestomathy*. Nevertheless, enough new information has been gleaned about Klingon that adding an addendum to the dictionary, even a brief one, seems beneficial.

In this addendum, the section-numbering system used in the main body of the dictionary is employed so that cross references may be easily made.

Once again, the author would like to thank the Federation Scientific Research Council for its support of this project, and, more importantly, would like to give credit to those who really make this effort possible: the increasing number of Klingons who are eager to share their language and culture with the rest of us. **taHjaj boq.**

3. NOUNS

3.3.1. Type 1: Noun Suffixes: Augmentative/diminutive

-oy *endearment*

This is an infrequently used, but nonetheless very interesting noun suffix. It is a very peculiar suffix because it is the only suffix that begins with a vowel rather than a consonant. (Though there are no examples, it is suspected that for those few nouns which end in a vowel, ' is inserted before this suffix.) The suffix usually follows a noun referring to a relative (*mother, father,* etc.), but it could also follow a noun for an animal, especially a pet, and means that the speaker is particularly fond of whatever the noun refers to. It is strongly suggested that non-native speakers of Klingon avoid this suffix unless they know what they are getting into.

vav *father*
be'nI' *sister*

vavoy *daddy*
be'nI'oy *sis*

4. VERBS

4.2.6. Type 6: Verb Suffixes: Qualification

-ba' *obviously*

This suffix is used when the speaker thinks that his or her assertion should be obvious to the listener. Nevertheless, there is still room for doubt; the suffix does not imply as strong a conviction as **-bej** *certainly*.

nepwI' Daba' *he/she is obviously lying* (**nepwI'** *liar,*
        Da *act in the manner of, behave as*)

4.2.9. Type 9: Verb Suffixes: Syntactic markers

-mo' *because*

This suffix is identical to the Type 5 noun suffix **-mo'** and has the same meaning, *due to, because of.*

bIganmo' *because you are old* (**gan** *be old*)
Heghpu'mo' yaS *because the officer died* (**Hegh** *die,*
        yaS *officer*)

-jaj *may*

This suffix is used to express a desire or wish on the part of the speaker that something take place in the future. When it is used, there is never a Type 7 aspect suffix. **-jaj** is often translated with *may* or *let*, and it is particularly useful when placing a curse or making a toast.

> **jaghpu'll' DaghIjjaj** *may you scare your enemies* (**jaghpu'll'** *your enemies*, **ghIj** *scare*)
>
> **tlhonchaj chIljaj** *may they lose their nostrils* (**tlhonchaj** *their nostrils*, **chIl** *lose*)

-ghach *nominalizer*

In Klingon, there are many instances of nouns and verbs being identical in form (e.g., **ta'** *accomplishment, accomplish*). It is not known if all verbs can be used as nouns, but it is known that verbs ending in suffixes (such as **-Ha'** *undo* in **lobHa'** *disobey*) can never be nouns. The Type 9 suffix **-ghach**, however, can be attached to such verbs in order to form nouns. Compare the following sets:

> **lo'** *use* (noun) (**lo'** *use, make use of*)
> **lo'laHghach** *value* (**lo'laH** *be valuable*)
> **lo'laHbe'ghach** *worthlessness* (**lo'laHbe'** *be worthless*)

> **naD** *commendation* (**naD** *commend*)
> **naDHa'ghach** *discommendation* (**naDHa'** *discommend*)
> **naDqa'gha'ch** *re-commendation* (**naDqa'** *commend again*)

5. OTHER KINDS OF WORDS

5.4. Adverbials

The list of adverbials given in the original dictionary can be expanded by the addition of the following:

ghaytan *likely*
jaS *differently*
nIteb *alone, acting alone, on one's own*
pe'vIl *forcefully*
SIbI' *immediately*

The earlier belief that adverbials come only at the beginning of sentences turns out to be not quite accurate. For a more correct description, see Section 6.7.

There is a second word (in addition to **neH** *only, merely*) which fits into this category despite its very peculiar behavior:

jay' *intensely*

This word not only intensifies whatever is being said, it turns the whole phrase into an invective. Alone among the adverbials, **jay'** always comes at the end of the sentence.

qaStaH nuq jay' *What the #$*@ is happening?*
          (**qaStaH** *it is occurring,* **nuq** *what?*)

mIch 'elpu' jay' *They've entered the #$%@ sector!*
        (mIch *sector,* 'elpu' *they've entered it*)

5.5 Exclamations

As it turns out, cursing is a fine art among Klingons. There
are many more curses than those three listed in the earlier
edition of the dictionary. It is not always clear how to use
the curses, but some are certainly epithetical (used for
name-calling), while others seem to have a more general
application. A few additional curses are listed below.

Epithets	General invective
petaQ	va
toDSaH	ghay'cha'
taHqeq	baQa'
yIntagh	Hu'tegh
Qovpatlh	

The invective **va** is actually just a shortened form of
Qu'vatlh. Note also that the adverbial **jay'** *intensely* is
invective in force (Section 5.4.).

6. SYNTAX

6.4. Questions

Tag questions (ending a statement with a question such as "right?" or "isn't that so?") are formed by using the verb **gar** *be accurate* plus the suffix **-'a'** *interrogative*. This word either follows the verb or else comes at the end of the sentence. Both of the following are correct:

De' Sov qar'a' HoD
De' Sov HoD qar'a' *The captain knows the information, right?* (**De'** *information*, **Sov** *he/she knows it*, **HoD** *captain*)

6.7. Placement of adverbial elements

It was earlier thought that all adverbials (except **neH** *only*) come at the beginning of the sentence. This is frequently the case, but what is really going on is that the adverbial precedes the object-verb-noun construction. It is possible for an element of another type to precede the adverb. Most commonly, this is a time element (a noun or phrase meaning *today, at six o'clock,* etc.).

DaHjaj nom Soppu' *Today they ate quickly* (**DaHjaj** *today*, **nom** *quickly*, **Soppu'** *they ate*)

179

The adverbial may actually follow the object noun (but still precede the verb) when the object noun is topicalized by means of the noun suffix -'e' (see Section 3.3.5.).

HaqwI' 'e' DaH yISam *Find the SURGEON now!*
(**HaqwI'** *surgeon,* **DaH** *now,* **yISam** *find him/her!*)

6.8. Indirect objects

While the object of the verb is the recipient of the action, the indirect object may be considered the beneficiary. In a Klingon sentence, the indirect object precedes the object and is suffixed with the Type 5 noun suffix **-vaD** *for, intended for.* The suffix may be attached to either a noun or a pronoun.

yaSvaD taj nobpu' qama' *The prisoner gave the officer the knife* (**yaS** *officer,* **taj** *knife,* **nobpu'** *gave,* **qama'** *prisoner*)

chaHvaD Soj qem yaS *The officer brings them food* (**chaH** *they,* **Soj** *food,* **qem** *bring,* **yaS** *officer*)

KLINGON-ENGLISH

bagh	tie (v)
beQ	be flat (v)
betleH	type of hand weapon (n)
bIj	punish (v)
bIj	punishment (n)
bIreQtagh	bregit lung (n)
boQ	aid, assistance (n)
chab	pie, tart, dumpling (n)
chIl	lose, misplace (v)
chov	assess, evaluate (v)
cho'	succession (n)
cho'	succeed (to authority) (v)
chuS'ugh	type of musical instrument (n)
chu'wI'	trigger (n)
Da	behave as, act in the manner of (v)
DaHjaj	today (n)
Daj	test inconclusively (v)
Daq	site, location (n)
Dargh	tea (n)
Degh	medal, emblem, symbol, insignia (n)
DI	litter, rubble, debris (n)
DoD	mark (in coordinates) (n)
DungluQ	noon (n)
Duy'a'	ambassador (n)
ghaytan	likely (adv)

ghew	bug, cootie (n)
ghe"or	netherworld (where dishonored go) (n)
ghoch	track, track down (v)
ghojmoq	nurse, nanny, governess (n)
ghuv	recruit (n)
Haqtaj	scalpel (n)
HaqwI'	surgeon (n)
Ha'DIbaH	meat, animal (n)
Hegh	death (n)
Hergh QaywI', HerghwI'	hypo, pneumatic hypo (n)
HIj	deliver, transport goods (v)
HoH	killing (n)
jaS	differently (adv)
jatlh	say (v)
jay'	intensely (invective) (adv)
ja'chuq	succession ritual (ancient) (n)
jech	disguise, costume (n)
jey	itinerary (n)
jIH	monitor (v)
jogh	quadrant (n)
juHqo'	home world (n)
lagh	ensign (n)
lagh	take apart, disassemble (v)
latlh	additional one, other one (n)
la'quv	Supreme Commander (n)
la"a'	commandant (n)
len	recess, break (n)
LeSSov	foresight (n)
lIngwI'	generator (n)
lo'	use (n)
lupDujHom	shuttlecraft (n)
lurgh	direction (spatial) (n)
mangHom	cadet (n)
matlh	be loyal (v)
mej	leave, depart (v)
meqba'	legal proceeding, type of (n)
mIw	procedure, process (n)
morgh	protest (v)
mun	intervene (v)

182

muvmoH	recruit (v)
muvtay	initiation (n)
nab	plan, procedure (n)
naD	praise, commend, approve (v)
naD	commendation (n)
naDHa'	discommend, disapprove (v)
naDHa'ghach	discommendation (n)
naH	fruit, vegetable (n)
naQ	be full, whole, entire (v)
naQ	cain, staff (n)
nargh	escape (v)
nejwI'	probe (n)
nenghep	Age of Ascension (n)
nentay	Rite of Ascension (n)
nImbuS wej	Nimbus III (n)
nIS	disrupt, interfere with (v)
nIteb	alone, acting alone (adv)
nItlhpach	fingernail (n)
noH	war (n)
notlh	be obsolete (v)
nuHmey	arsenal (n)
nuqjatlh	what did you say?
	huh? what? (excl)
ngeHbej	cosmos (n)
ngoch	policy (n)
pach	claw (n)
patlh	rank (military, governmental) (n)
peHghep	Age of Inclusion (n)
peQ	magnetism (n)
peQ chem	magnetic field (n)
pe'vIl	forcefully, by force (adv)
pIn'a'	master (n)
pIpyuS	pipius (n)
pIw	odor (n)
pop	reward (n)
potlh	be important (v)
qaD	challenge (n)
qaD	challenge (v)
qagh	serpent worm (as food) (n)
qaq	be preferable (v)
qar	be accurate (v)

qawHaq	data banks (singular) (n)
qel	consider, take into account (v)
qIt	be possible (v)
qo'	world, realm (n)
qughDuj	cruiser (n)
qumwI'	governor (n)
qutluch	type of hand weapon (n)
quv	honor (n)
quv	be honored (v)
quvmoH	honor (v)
QaH	help (n)
Qang	chancellor (n)
QI'tomer	Khitomer (n)
QI'tu'	Paradise (n)
Qol	beam away (v)
Qo'	no, I disagree (excl)
Qo'noS	Kronos (n)
ra'ghomquv	High Command (n)
rI'	hail (v)
rI'Se'	hailing frequency (n)
ro'qegh'Iwchab	rokeg blood pie (n)
ruch	proceed, go ahead, do it (v)
rura' pente'	Rura Penthe (n)
ruStay	bonding ritual (n)
Sam	locate, seek and find (v)
sIbI'	immediately (adv)
Sogh	lieutenant (n)
Soj	food (n)
SonchIy	death ritual (for a leader) (n)
Sov	knowledge (n)
SuD	gamble, take a chance, take a risk (v)
Sugh	install (in office) (v)
SuvwI'	warrior (n)
tagh	lung (n)
tagh	begin a process, initiate (v)
taH	continue, go on, endure (v)
targh	targ (n)
tay	ceremony, rite, ritual (n)
tob	test conclusively, prove (v)
toD	rescue (n)

toDuj	courage, bravery (n)
toQDuj	Bird of Prey (vessel) (n)
totlh	commodore (n)
toy'wI''a'	slave (n)
tlham	gravity (n)
tlhIj	apologize (v)
tlhIlHal	mine (n)
tlhIngan Hubbeq	Klingon Defense Force (n)
tlhob	request, ask, plead (v)
tlho'	appreciation, gratitude (n)
tlho'	thank (v)
vaj	warrior (n)
van	salute, tribute (n)
van'a'	award (n)
vaq	mock (v)
vaS	hall, assembly hall (n)
vaS'a'	Great Hall (n)
veH tIn	Great Barrier (n)
veqlargh	devil, demon, Fek'lhr (n)
verengan	Ferengi (n)
veSDuj	warship (n)
vID	be belligerent (v)
vIH	move, be in motion (v)
vIt	truth (n)
vI'	sharpshooting, marksmanship (n)
weQ	candle (n)
woj	radiation (n)
woj choHwI'	reactor (n)
wuq	decide upon (v)
yagh	organism (n)
yaH	be taken away (v)
yejquv	High Council (n)
'aH	paraphernalia (n)
'aj	admiral (n)
'ech	brigadier (n)
'evnagh	subspace (n)
'oD	arbitrate, mediate (v)
'otlh	photon (n)
'oy'naQ	painstick (n)

ENGLISH-KLINGON

accurate, be accurate (v)	qar
act in the manner of, behave as (v)	Da
additional one, other one (n)	latlh
admiral (n)	'aj
Age of Ascension (n)	nenghep
Age of Inclusion (n)	peHghep
aid, assistance (n)	boQ
alone, acting alone (adv)	nIteb
ambassador (n)	Duy'a'
apologize (v)	tlhIj
appreciation, gratitude (n)	tlho'
approve, commend, praise (v)	naD
arbitrate, mediate (v)	'oD
arsenal (n)	nuHmey
assess, evaluate (v)	chov
award (n)	van'a'
beam away (v)	Qol
begin a process, initiate (v)	tagh
behave as, act in the manner of (v)	Da
belligerent, be belligerent (v)	vID
Bird of Prey (vessel) (n)	toQDuj
bonding ritual (n)	ruStay
break, recess (n)	len
bregit lung (n)	bIreQtagh
brigadier (n)	'ech

bug, cootie (n)	ghew
cadet (n)	mangHom
cain, staff (n)	naQ
candle (n)	weQ
ceremony, rite, ritual (n)	tay
challenge (v)	qaD
challenge (n)	qaD
chance, take a chance, gamble (v)	SuD
chancellor (n)	Qang
claw (n)	pach
commandant (n)	la"a'
commend, approve, praise (v)	naD
commendation (n)	naD
commodore (n)	totlh
complete, be complete, whole (v)	naQ
consider, take into account (v)	qel
continue, go on, endure (v)	taH
cosmos (n)	ngeHbej
costume, disguise (n)	jech
courage, bravery (n)	toDuj
cruiser (n)	qughDuj
data banks (singular) (n)	qawHaq
death (n)	Hegh
death ritual (for a leader) (n)	SonchIy
debris, litter, rubble (n)	DI
decide upon (v)	wuq
deliver, transport goods (v)	HIj
devil, demon, Fek'lhr (n)	veqlargh
differently (adv)	jaS
direction (spatial) (n)	lurgh
disassemble, take apart (v)	lagh
discommend, disapprove (v)	naDHa'
discommendation (n)	naDHa'ghach
disguise, costume (n)	jech
disrupt, interfere with (v)	nIS
emblem, symbol, medal, insignia (n)	Degh
endure, continue, go on (v)	taH
ensign (n)	lagh
escape (v)	nargh
evaluate, assess (v)	chov

Ferengi (n)	verengan
fingernail (n)	nItlhpach
flat, be flat (v)	beQ
food (n)	Soj
forcefully, by force (adv)	pe'vIl
foresight (n)	leSSov
fruit, vegetable (n)	naH
full, be full, whole, entire (v)	naQ
gamble, take a chance, take a risk (v)	SuD
generator (n)	lIngwI'
governess, nurse, nanny (n)	ghojmoq
governor (n)	qumwI'
gratitude, appreciation (n)	tlho'
gravity (n)	tlham
Great Hall (n)	vaS'a'
Great Barrier (n)	veH tIn
hail (v)	rI'
hailing frequency (n)	rI'Se'
hall, assembly hall (n)	vaS
help (n)	QaH
High Council (n)	yejquv
High Command (n)	ra'ghomquv
home world (n)	juHqo'
honor (n)	quv
honor (v)	quvmoH
honored, be honored (v)	quv
hypo, pneumatic hypo (n)	Hergh QaywI', HerghwI'
immediately (adv)	sIbI'
important, be important (v)	potlh
initiate proceedings, begin process (v)	tagh
initiation (n)	muvtay
install (in office) (v)	Sugh
intensely (invective) (adv)	jay'
interfere with, disrupt (v)	nIS
intervene (v)	mun
itinerary (n)	jey
Khitomer (n)	QI'tomer
killing (n)	HoH

Klingon Defense Force (n)	tlhIngan Hubbeq
knowledge (n)	Sov
Kronos (n)	Qo'noS
leave, depart (v)	mej
legal proceeding, type of (n)	meqba'
lieutenant (n)	Sogh
likely (adv)	ghaytan
litter, rubble, debris (n)	DI
locate, seek and find (v)	Sam
location, site (n)	Daq
lose, misplace (v)	chIl
loyal, be loyal (v)	matlh
lung (n)	tagh
magnetic field (n)	peQ chem
magnetism (n)	peQ
mark (in coordinates) (n)	DoD
marksmanship, sharpshooting (n)	vI'
master (n)	pIn'a'
meat, animal (n)	Ha'DIbaH
medal, emblem, symbol, insignia (n)	Degh
mediate, arbitrate (v)	'oD
mine (n)	tlhIlHal
mock (v)	vaq
monitor (v)	jIH
move, be in motion (v)	vIH
musical instrument, type of (n)	chuS'ugh
netherworld (where dishonored go) (n)	ghe''or
Nimbus III (n)	nImbuS wej
no, I disagree (excl)	Qo'
noon (n)	DungluQ
nurse, nanny, governess (n)	ghojmoq
obsolete, be obsolete (v)	notlh
odor (n)	pIw
organism (n)	yagh
other one, additional one (n)	latlh
painstick (n)	'oy'naQ
Paradise (n)	QI'tu'
paraphernalia (n)	'aH

photon (n)	'otlh
pie, tart, dumpling (n)	chab
pipius (n)	pIpyuS
plan, procedure (n)	nab
policy (n)	ngoch
possible, be possible (v)	qIt
praise, commend, approve (v)	naD
preferable, be preferable (v)	qaq
probe (n)	nejwI'
procedure, process (n)	mIw
proceed, go ahead, do it (v)	ruch
protest (v)	morgh
punish (v)	bIj
punishment (n)	bIj
quadrant (n)	jogh
radiation (n)	woj
rank (military, governmental) (n)	patlh
reactor (n)	woj choHwI'
realm, world (n)	qo'
recess, break (n)	len
recruit (n)	ghuv
recruit (v)	muvmoH
request, ask, plead (v)	tlhob
rescue (n)	toD
reward (n)	pop
risk, take a risk, take a chance (v)	SuD
rite, ritual, ceremony (n)	tay
Rite of Ascension (n)	nentay
rokeg blood pie (n)	ro'qegh'Iwchab
Rura Penthe (n)	rura' pente'
salute, tribute (n)	van
say (v)	jatlh
scalpel (n)	Haqtaj
seek and find, locate (v)	Sam
serpent worm (as food) (n)	qagh
sharpshooting, marksmanship (n)	vI'
shuttlecraft (n)	lupDujHom
site, location (n)	Daq
slave (n)	toy'wI''a'
subspace (n)	'evnagh
succeed (to authority) (v)	cho'

succession (n)	cho'
succession ritual (ancient) (n)	ja'chuq
Supreme Commander (n)	la'quv
surgeon (n)	HaqwI'
take apart, disassemble (v)	lagh
taken away, be taken away (v)	yaH
targ (n)	targh
tart, pie, dumpling (n)	chab
tea (n)	Dargh
test conclusively, prove (v)	tob
test inconclusively (v)	Daj
thank (v)	tlho'
tie (v)	bagh
today (n)	DaHjaj
track, track down (v)	ghoch
traitor (n)	'urwI'
transport goods, deliver (v)	HIj
treason, commit treason (v)	'ur
tribute, salute (n)	van
trigger (n)	chu'wI'
truth (n)	vIt
use (n)	lo'
vegetable, fruit (n)	naH
war (n)	noH
warrior (n)	SuvwI', vaj
warship (n)	veSDuj
weapon:	qutluch, betleH
types of hand weapons (n)	
what did you say?	nuqjatlh
huh? what? (excl)	
whole, be whole, full, entire (v)	naQ
world, realm (n)	qo'